A WITCH IN TIME

Ralph's uncle was different somehow from other people's uncles. For a start, there were those striking eyes—grey and green and deep as the deepest lake—that seemed to see right into you. As Ralph explained to Maddy, with Uncle Alistair in charge anything might happen. And right next door, just over the wall, was a mysterious new neighbour, Mrs Morgan, whose sinister figure cast no shadow—no shadow at all.

Dark magic is in the air in this spine-chilling story. As the mystery unfolds, events move rapidly towards the heart-stopping climax. Maddy, Ralph and his uncle stand alone and apparently defenceless against Mrs Morgan's terrible powers—yet always watching, guarding, is the grandfather clock, with its measured tick and timeless promise.

WILLIAM RAEPER has written a number of books including a collection of fairy tales, *The Troll and the Butterfly*, and a biography of one of the greatest storytellers of all, George MacDonald. He lives and works in Oxford, in between his travels to other countries—from Norway to Nepal.

A WITCH IN TIME

WILLIAM RAEPER

A LION PAPERBACK

Oxford · Batavia · Sydney

Copyright © 1992 William Raeper

Published by
Lion Publishing plc
Sandy Lane West, Oxford, England
ISBN 0 7459 2073 X
Albatross Books Pty Ltd
PO Box 320, Sutherland, NSW 2232, Australia
ISBN 0 7324 0521 1

First edition 1992

A catalogue record for this book is available
from the British Library

Printed and bound in Great Britain

And God said:
*   'Whenever the rainbow appears in the clouds,*
*   I will see it*
*   and remember the everlasting covenant*
*   between God and all living creatures*
*   of every kind*
*   on the earth.'*

Genesis, chapter 9, verse 16

1

'Are you ready, Ralph?' asked Ralph's mother, quickly buttoning up her coat.

'Yes,' replied Ralph through a mouthful of chocolate biscuit. Ralph's mother tutted and looked agitated. It was one of her favourite looks, especially when she was in a hurry, and today she was in an especial hurry.

'And he hasn't arrived yet,' she muttered, much more to herself than to Ralph. 'The taxi will be here in a minute. Go and look out of the window.' As though that would bring him any quicker. Ralph went to have a look.

'Any sign yet?'

'No,' mumbled Ralph. He took another bite out of his chocolate biscuit. But then, he wasn't going. For once he was staying.

Ralph lived in a town where most of the houses were large and built of red bricks. There was a railway station at the north end and a bus station and a long street full of shops—the same shops you find in any town. Ralph's father, who had a scratchy beard and smoked a pipe, was a schoolteacher. Ralph's mother taught the piano to some of his father's pupils who came to the house, but, for the most part she looked after the twins, who were a year old and screamed a lot. Two babies, instead of the expected one, meant twice the noise on top of everything else.

Ralph and his family lived in the top half of a big house overlooking the cricket pitch of the school where Ralph's father taught. The road outside their house was narrow—

two cars could hardly scrape by each other—and it was lined with trees. In the distance (on the days when you could see them) were some low hills, hills that showed you the difference between the earth and the sky.

It was the Easter holidays now, though all the family's plans had been completely disarranged owing to sudden and unforeseen circumstances. Ralph's father had taken the twins off on holiday a couple of days early to give Ralph's mother a break. They were at Aunt Judith's. Ralph and his mother were getting ready to join them—when—there was a phone call.

Ralph had heard the phone ring and had gone into the hall. He watched his mother twisting the cord and half hiding her face so that Ralph could not hear what she was saying. Granny was ill. Granny up in Scotland. She was not too ill. But ill.

'Yes, of course—I'll come as soon as I can,' insisted Ralph's mother, and hung up. But how? She and Ralph were due to leave the following day. For a week. And there was Ralph's father at Aunt Judith's with the twins. Ralph's mother went into the kitchen to put the kettle on for a cup of tea. That helped her think sometimes, giving her something to do. She thumped her fist on the kitchen table in frustration and said out loud, 'Oh, I do wish something would happen to help me!'—just as the kettle was beginning to whistle. The steam and scream of the kettle filled the kitchen and clouded the windows— when—there was another ring at the phone.

'Bother!' expostulated Ralph's mother, switching off the gas. 'Who can it be this time? Bad news once in a day is quite enough.' Ralph was in the living-room with some of his track laid out. He was busy with his trains and was just about to get his 125 moving when he heard his mother answer: 'Hello—oh, Alistair, it's you. Where are you?'

It was Uncle Alistair. Ralph's ears pricked up like a dog's. Uncle Alistair.

Ralph sat up cross-legged in the middle of the living-room and tried to listen to as much of his mother's conversation as possible. For Ralph's uncle was different somehow from other people's uncles. Ralph's uncle had lived for a long time in Africa and had a huge house full of the things he had brought back from there. There was something about him . . . Ralph remembered his uncle's striking eyes—grey and green with no bottom to them, like a deep, deep lake—and how they seemed to see, not right through you, but right into you.

Ralph wondered what his Uncle Alistair wanted. He was so rarely at home; always away in some country or other, always doing things that he never could—no never *would*—properly explain. He was always up to something.

'You've heard, then?' said Ralph's mother. There was a pause. 'Well, that's very kind of you. I mean, I thought I would take Ralph up with me for a week—or else tie a label to him and send him off on his own to join his father. Yes, I know you can't be too careful. But—are you sure? I didn't think children were quite your line. Well, if you've got some research to do as well. Hold on, I'll ask him. Then he can't pretend that I've ordered him to do anything. Ralph!' Ralph's mother cupped her hand over the phone receiver and leaned round the living-room door. 'It's your Uncle Alistair on the phone.'

'Really?' said Ralph innocently, straightening up and running a hand through his sandy hair.

'He has offered—kindly offered—to come here and stay with you for a week while I go up to Granny's to look after her. Would you like that—or do you want to come up with me?'

Ralph wrinkled his nose and pretended to think for a moment. He had, of course, already decided, but he did not want his mother to see that.

'I'll stay here,' he nodded firmly.

9

'You sure?' asked his mother. 'You won't change your mind?'

'I'm sure!' shouted Ralph, jumping to his feet and whirling his arms round like an aeroplane.

Ralph's mother tutted and spoke into the phone. 'He's sure—about you, that is. I'm not, though. But anyway—can you come tomorrow morning? Ten o'clock. There's a train. Are *you* sure, now? Very well, then.' Ralph's mother put the phone down and just stood there for a moment. She was very puzzled. It was not at all like her mysterious brother to ring up out of the blue and offer to come and look after children—well, one child, and his nephew at that, but even so. There must be more to this than met the eye. But how could there possibly be? By now she had quite forgotten her tea. She walked into the living-room where Ralph had started whizzing one of his trains round the track again. His 125.

'Your Uncle Alistair's coming at ten o'clock tomorrow—for a week. I think there's a train at half past, so I'll be going pretty quickly. Now, what was I going to do? Oh, yes—tea, I need it! And then I must phone your father.'

The taxi was due. Uncle Alistair had still not arrived. Ralph's mother was doing last-minute things to her hair in the bathroom when the door-bell rang. 'Is that him, Ralph? You go down. I look a sight.'

Ralph opened the front door. But it wasn't Uncle Alistair and it wasn't the taxi driver.

'Hello,' said Ralph.

It was Maddy. Maddy was Ralph's friend who lived two streets away with her mother. She came round often, though she didn't like trains very much. They were in the same class at school. Like Ralph she was wearing jeans and a T-shirt, but her hair was a bit redder than the shade of Ralph's sand and she was a bit taller. She sat down in the hall and took off her mucky trainers—a rule in Ralph's house.

'Who is it?' bustled Ralph's mother at the top of the stair. 'Oh, Maddy, it's you. I thought you were the taxi driver. Or my brother. My very late brother. Now, where's my handbag?' Ralph's mother had already put her case down in the hall.

'What's going on?' asked Maddy as she tugged at her laces.

'Dad's away, Granny's ill,' explained Ralph, 'and Uncle Alistair's coming to look after me for a week.'

'Uncle Alistair—who's he?'

'He's... he's... well, he's my uncle!' Ralph struggled and failed to find the right words. He tried to paint a picture of his uncle in his mind, so as to be able to tell Maddy what he was like—but it was difficult. Uncle Alistair was someone you felt, rather than someone you saw. Ralph remembered his uncle's eyes again.

'He's... he's... different!' pronounced Ralph firmly, and that was the nearest he got to what he wanted to say, for then, at the door, came an almighty knock.

'At last!' exclaimed Ralph's mother in relief as she ran down the stairs and opened the door. Uncle Alistair smiled and gave her a reassuring hug.

'Hello, Ralph,' he said, looking down on Ralph as though from a great height. It was odd, Ralph thought, how Uncle Alistair always appeared to be taller than he actually was—that is, if you measured him you would have found that he was smaller than you had remembered. 'And who is this?'

'Maddy,' said Ralph.

'Hello, Maddy,' smiled Uncle Alistair.

'Hello,' said Maddy shyly, getting up quickly and standing very straight.

'You said ten o'clock,' scolded Ralph's mother.

'The train was late,' replied Uncle Alistair easily. He had

11

an old, knocked-about suitcase with him, and he was wearing a grey jacket and smart trousers. There was something crisp and clear about him: his well-defined movements matched his clothes.

'I think,' continued Uncle Alistair, 'that I would like a little tea. As I recall, tea flows very freely in this house.'

'You'll have to get it yourself,' returned Ralph's mother. 'I . . .' Outside in the road a horn tooted brashly two or three times. 'That's my taxi! Now, you will be good, won't you, Ralph?' said his mother, kissing him on the cheek.

'But will I?' teased Uncle Alistair with a smile.

'You'd better be,' ordered Ralph's mother. 'I want no wild happenings in this house while I'm gone!' The horn tooted again. 'Goodbye! Goodbye, Maddy! Goodbye!' Ralph's mother hurried to the front door, down the front steps, out of the gate, and into the taxi.

'Do you think she'll be late?' asked Ralph.

'No,' answered Uncle Alistair, shaking his head slightly. 'Besides, her train's not on time.'

'How do you know?' asked Maddy. But Uncle Alistair did not explain.

'Let's wave goodbye! I'll race you!' Ralph and Maddy ran up the stairs and through to the living-room window, pressing their faces flat against it. They watched as the taxi negotiated the narrow road and turned the corner out of sight.

'Well, now,' declared Uncle Alistair, joining them from the kitchen with a mug of tea in his hand. 'That is that.'

The sun burst out from behind one of the big, puffy clouds that were moored but shifting gently in the harbour of the sky like great ships. Sunlight swept along the street with the fresh, bracing wind blowing the heads of the trees and throwing their shadows down onto the ground.

'I do believe it's going to be fine after all,' decided Uncle

Alistair. 'Maybe you two can show me around after lunch.'

'Show you where?' asked Maddy.

'Anywhere,' replied Uncle Alistair. He sat down in the armchair that had its back to the big cupboard. 'I've been to this house before, but I can't say that I have ever really been to this town. Perhaps later today—if the weather holds—we can indulge in a little—ah—*exploration*.' He said the last word as though he had been waiting to taste it for a long time.

'Fine,' shrugged Ralph, 'but,' he stood close to Maddy and looked squarely at his uncle, 'you don't want to see the shops, do you?' Ralph had a horror of shops. Especially of shopping for shoes with his mother.

'No!' laughed Uncle Alistair. 'I don't want to see the shops, but I do want to see . . . everything else . . . that is, everything you want to show me.'

'Shall we make a plan?' suggested Maddy.

'Oh, no, no plans!' interrupted Uncle Alistair hastily. 'Plans just spoil things. If you want something to happen, you must never make a plan. That's the first and most important rule.'

'And what's the second?' asked Ralph. He had forgotten how green his uncle's eyes were. And now, although he was sitting there in the chair, his eyes had a distant, faraway look. His uncle, however, snapped back to the present in a flash.

'The second and most important rule, is to see what there is in the kitchen. Are you coming?' Ralph's uncle rose and smoothed his trousers. 'The kitchen,' he informed them, 'is always the most exciting room in the house.' He chuckled slightly to himself and led the way.

Ralph's kitchen was small, but big enough to eat in. There was a gas cooker and a sink, a tall dresser with plates arranged on it, and cupboards above and below the long, smooth working surface that lay at right angles to the

13

kitchen window. Where there were hills at the front of the house, at the back there were houses and new flats, all crowded together. The house Ralph lived in, however, had a square garden, neatly planted with roses.

They shared the house with Mr Patterson who lived downstairs—an old man who was chaplain at the school where Ralph's father worked. He was friendly enough, but Ralph sometimes thought he preferred roses to children—and sometimes his dog could howl even louder than the twins. He was away this week, though, visiting one of his daughters. Next door, over the wall, was another house—not divided up like Ralph's—and a woman hanging out her washing in the garden. For a moment, Ralph thought he saw a cloud pass over his uncle's face.

'Surely not!' Uncle Alistair said to himself. Lifting the turquoise curtain, he stood sideways to the kitchen window and stared out. The woman had almost emptied her basket and had thrown a long, white nightgown over the line. There was a strange rusty stain on it that had not quite come out in the wash.

'Who is she?' asked Uncle Alistair, with a bewildering note of warning in his voice.

'Oh, *her!*' snorted Maddy, sitting down with elbows on the kitchen table, and head between her fists.

'That's Mrs Morgan,' said Ralph.

'And?' said Uncle Alistair, inviting Ralph to go on.

'She's new,' continued Ralph. 'She's only been living there for a couple of weeks.'

'And she's not very friendly,' added Maddy. 'My friend's ball went into her garden and she wouldn't give it him back. She just shouted at him.'

'And when Mr Patterson's dog Bathsheba saw her in the street, she barked and barked—Bathsheba, that is, not Mrs Morgan.'

'I get the picture,' interrupted Uncle Alistair before

14

Maddy and Ralph could say anything more about their new and unwelcome neighbour.

'Let me look,' said Ralph, moving to the window. The wind was blowing and the April sun, watery and inconstant, had bathed all the houses in momentary light. It was shining very oddly on Mrs Morgan's teeth. They glittered so. Ralph's stomach tightened, but it must just be his imagination. When you said things, sometimes it made you see things that weren't really there. Mrs Morgan's teeth! He was just being stupid.

'I'll tell you one thing about her that is strange,' said Uncle Alistair in a quiet voice, almost as though he were answering Ralph's thoughts.

Maddy lifted her head and Ralph turned away from the window to look at his uncle. 'What's that?' he asked.

Uncle Alistair raised his eyebrows. 'She doesn't cast a shadow. Look, look closely, there's nothing there at all!'

2

No shadow. No shadow. The sun passed behind a cloud and the conversation turned to other things.

Lunch was toasted sandwiches which came out of the toaster in queer, squidgy shapes.

'I never was much good with machines,' apologized Uncle Alistair with a frown. He dropped one of the hot sandwiches onto a plate and passed it to Maddy. 'Here you are, eat up.'

'Thanks,' said Maddy, looking at the object on her plate in an unconvinced kind of a way. She and Ralph munched, while Uncle Alistair searched in the cupboards till he found a plastic bottle of concentrated orange juice. He measured it into three beakers, filled them with water from the tap, and set them on the table. Then he sat down, sipped his juice and ate a little of his sandwich. 'It's... different,' he remarked with a laugh.

'I think everything's different today,' returned Ralph.

'Oh, no,' said Uncle Alistair, putting both hands behind his head and stretching, 'everything is always the same—it's only when you look at things closely that you see how different they are.' He yawned. Then, 'Where are you going to take me?'

'I don't know,' said Ralph. 'Out.'

'Out it is,' laughed Uncle Alistair. 'Out is a very big place, though, and it's cold today even if the sun is shining, so wrap up warmly.'

As Ralph and Maddy put on their warm jackets, Ralph

16

kept wondering about Mrs Morgan next door. No shadow. It was, well—odd to say the least. And he hadn't noticed it before. Not until Uncle Alistair had pointed it out. Was that what he had meant about looking closely?

'Ready?' asked Maddy, already zipped up.

'Sure,' said Ralph.

'Race you, then,' challenged Maddy. And they thundered and stumbled down the stairs to the door, breathing hard and shaking the framed pictures that were fixed none too well to the wall.

'Quiet, you two!' yelled Uncle Alistair from above. 'It sounds as if you're trying to knock the house down! What will the neighbours think?'

'Mr Patterson's away. The neighbours can't hear us!' shouted Ralph.

'Except Mrs Morgan,' added Maddy. 'I bet she can hear everything.'

'And maybe she can,' said Uncle Alistair, moving easily down the stairs. 'Now, where's the key to this house? I don't want your mother to come home to find we've been burgled.'

At the bottom of the stairs there was a square sort of hall. It wasn't really a hall, just a bit of the house left over after it had been divided in two. There was an upright piano against one wall, a window, then the vacuum cleaner and some brooms. The floorboards were bare. Coats were piled on the post at the bottom of the banister, there were shoes and wellingtons in a ragged line on an old newspaper, and there was a grandfather clock.

'What a fine clock,' admired Uncle Alistair, catching its well-measured tick. It was tall, wooden and well-polished. Its glass face shone in the April sunlight and, painted near the bottom of the face, there was a rainbow. 'Most extraordinary!' pronounced Uncle Alistair as he peered at it closely. 'I wonder how that came to be here?'

17

'It was Granny's,' explained Ralph. 'Don't you remember? She gave it to us when she moved to a smaller house. She didn't like it very much—she always thought the clock was watching her.'

'Guarding, guarding,' murmured Uncle Alistair. 'It's amazing how these things turn up.' And then, in a louder voice, 'Yes, I thought I had seen it before, but I couldn't remember. I was away when your grandmother moved—somewhere in India, I think. Now, let's find what Out has in store for us. After you,' and he gave a mock bow to let Maddy and Ralph out of the house before him and down the steps to the gate.

'There's the cathedral,' said Ralph, pointing through the cold air at the high, impressive building.

'Most interesting,' said Uncle Alistair.

'Is it?' Ralph hunched his shoulders and stuck his hands in his pockets.

'Ah,' said Uncle Alistair, 'you shouldn't despise what you don't understand. There's more to cathedrals than stones and statues and organs. They're here for a reason.'

Ralph and Maddy followed Uncle Alistair unwillingly as he led them up to the great cathedral door. Neither of them really wanted to go any further. There was a notice pinned just inside about a local schools' painting competition. Noah and the animals—Noah and the animals and the rainbow that was a promise at the end of the story. Boards stuck with pictures splashed with animals and rainbows filled one of the wall aisles of the cathedral. Under the high, dusty statues inside hung a banner, sewn in bright colours: 'I have set my rainbow in the clouds,' it said, 'and it will be the sign of the covenant between me and the earth.' A covenant was a promise. Maddy knew that from school. And rainbows. There had been a lot of rain recently, but no rainbows.

'Do we have to go in?' asked Ralph.

After a moment Uncle Alistair relented. 'All right. You win. Maybe, as today's an Out kind of day, we shouldn't begin by going In straight away. In should always come after Out. That's the proper way of things.'

'There's the river,' Ralph suggested in relief. 'That's Out.'

'Oh, very Out,' agreed Uncle Alistair. 'Let's start there.' So the three of them left the cathedral and set off down the street, past red-brick houses, solid under their grey slate roofs. They passed the post office and the grocer's. They crossed the road close to the school where Ralph's father worked, and turned towards the river. Maddy and Ralph ran ahead to the gate of the river path, stopping to let Uncle Alistair catch up, and pointing things out to him.

'The meadows are over there,' waved Ralph, 'but we want to go the other way, down to the water.' Maddy and Uncle Alistair followed close behind as Ralph led them down the path that led to the river's edge. The water was flowing so fast it was foaming. So fast, that it was hard to see how the ducks could swim against the current. But they did, turning sideways and holding close to the bank. Tourists with cameras strolled by, and parents with prams. One or two tramps sat on the benches, muttering and holding tight their half-empty cider bottles. Ralph, Maddy and Uncle Alistair followed the edge of the rushing water for a long way, until they finally came to the big stone bridge which brought the cars into the centre of town.

'Let's go up here,' said Uncle Alistair.

'That only goes into town,' warned Maddy.

'To the shops,' said Ralph, with a half-accusing expression on his face.

'I don't want to go to the shops,' protested Uncle Alistair. 'But if I were going to an ice-cream shop, you wouldn't complain.'

'No, I wouldn't,' laughed Ralph. Then he paused. 'Are

19

you going to an ice-cream shop?'

'If you like,' said Uncle Alistair, 'but it's a bit cold for ice-cream. If someone could invent warm ice-cream for days like this, that would be much better.' Already he was striding up the road that led back into town. Further along, the main road split into two, round the base of a statue of an old English king who stood resolutely on a bank of green. The statue was huge and had far too much writing at the bottom of it for Ralph to read. On the left of them was a tourist information centre in an old stone building decked with tiny turrets and pillars, while across the street, up some steps, there was a sign that announced MUSEUM.

'What about there?' asked Uncle Alistair.

'Oh, NO!' wailed Maddy and Ralph almost together. 'Not a museum! They're so boring!'

'Give it a chance,' said Uncle Alistair. 'If you really don't like it, we can come out again. I'd just like a peek at what they've got.'

'All right,' agreed Ralph is a grudging voice, as though he were granting his uncle a favour. Maddy pulled a long face and grunted. They waited for the traffic to part on the main road before crossing. 'NOW!' yelled Uncle Alistair as they plunged off the pavement.

The sky had greyed now, and all the shadows had gone back to wherever shadows go to. It was that time of the day when shopping comes to an end and people go home to warm, lit houses, and television and something good to eat. The museum had only fifteen minutes left till it closed.

'There isn't anybody else here,' complained Ralph. 'Look!'

Uncle Alistair poked his head into the doorway of the museum. Like the tourist information office it was in an old, converted building. The museum was probably just going to be two or three rooms filled with boring glass cases.

'Hello,' greeted a voice. It came from a man in glasses and a tweed jacket who was standing smoking a pipe. 'Visitors? We haven't had many of those today. The museum's about to close.'

'I want to take these two in to have a look,' explained Uncle Alistair, 'but it's proving a struggle. What is there?'

'Hmm,' the man sucked at his pipe. 'There's the special exhibition upstairs. That's worth seeing. You should go and look at that. Down here there are only stuffed animals and old photographs with a bit of history of the town. Upstairs is definitely more interesting.' Smoke rose from his pipe and tumbled out of his nostrils, making the air blue.

Uncle Alistair turned to Maddy and Ralph. 'Upstairs!' he ordered. 'Two minutes if you don't like it, fifteen if you do!'

Reluctantly, Maddy and Ralph grabbed hold of the wooden banister and began to climb the stairs.

'What's the exhibition?' asked Uncle Alistair.

'Books,' puffed the curator. Uncle Alistair looked around. There was a till and counter in the hallway with books and calendars and leaflets on it. Posters were stuck to the walls and there was a revolving stand of postcards.

'Books? I don't think they're going to like that.'

'Ah, but these are special books.' The curator's voice was almost conspiratorial. 'They came originally from Melton Abbey—the ruins are still to be seen, but it was closed and destroyed by Henry the Eighth. The Abbey was noted for its treasury of unusual books, all copied out by hand by the generations of monks who lived there, and beautifully illuminated.'

'That's very interesting,' remarked Uncle Alistair thoughtfully, glancing upstairs and listening for the expected howls of disgust.

'But they were all swiped centuries back.'

'Swiped?'

'The books. Tch! My pipe's gone out—it's a new one.'
Blinking through his thick, plastic-rimmed spectacles, the
man searched in his jacket pocket for a box of matches.

'Who—er—swiped them?' asked Uncle Alistair with
some interest.

'For a long time nobody knew, though some suspected.
It turned out the books had been swiped by Lord Marchbury who lived at the big house on Cookham Hill, just
outside of town. But nobody knew.'

'Nobody knew till when?'

'Till last year. The last of the Marchbury family was an
old lady: lived in the house for most of her life with a
cousin of hers. They were the last—no relatives worth
speaking of. Well, when the old lady died she left her
house to the National Trust—and what a treasure-trove
they found. Then, to cap it all, in a sealed room in the
basement they came across the books we've got on
display upstairs, all stowed away in some locked chests.
No one knew anything about them. Probably nobody had
even laid eyes on them for a few hundred years.'

'How exciting,' said Uncle Alistair. In the gathering
gloom, he felt something deep inside him beginning to
stir.

'They were too valuable to leave in the house, of
course, and the council wanted to keep them here. But
they're off to the British Museum soon for safe-keeping,
till a proper home can be found for them. So, ours is the
first exhibition, though it's only a temporary one.' The
man had spoken so much that he had forgotten about his
pipe—but then he remembered and struck a match. The
tobacco burned red in the end of his pipe once again. From
upstairs came the stamp of hurried feet.

'Oh, no,' thought Uncle Alistair to himself, 'they've had
enough already.'

'Uncle Alistair! Uncle Alistair!' shouted Ralph from the
top of the stair.

'Come and look! Quickly!'

'Just a moment,' said Uncle Alistair to the curator, excusing himself. 'I really must go and have a look, or you'll be closing.'

The curator waved his pipe at Uncle Alistair in kindly dismissal, and Uncle Alistair went to climb the stairs. His slim feet made no noise on the rackety steps.

'Here! They're in here!' urged Ralph insistently, pulling at his uncle's arm. The door to the exhibition room was dark green and hung open. An old radiator gurgled against the wall. White, creamy blinds were half drawn down the high windows, and the floor was wooden boards and shiny.

'You can slide,' said Maddy, demonstrating. The room had the keen clear smell of polish that ran right up your nostrils and right down into your lungs. The collection of glass cases seemed to quiver in the yellow brightness of the lamps, while the grey light from outside gave everything a ghostly sheen.

'Look!' said Ralph. 'Look!'

Around the walls stood a row of cases on legs, like desks with glass lids. Some of the books were laid out inside them and fixed invisibly. Most were Bibles or psalteries—some showed the beginning of a Gospel or an epistle, lavishly illustrated in different colours. One was a short psalm bearing the artist's idea of Jerusalem. There was also a medical book with drawings of herbs and parts of animals to be used for various sicknesses. But it was written in Latin, so neither Maddy nor Ralph could make head nor tail of it.

'It's this one I don't understand,' said Maddy, skipping over to a glass case in the centre of the room—one of the ones you could walk all round. Uncle Alistair stepped quickly to Maddy's side and, as he did so, he felt ... a disturbance. He had felt it before—something he recognized instantly.

The book Maddy was interested in was almost upright on a stand inside the display case and was much larger than the other books. It was open at two pages on which were written what seemed to be two short poems in Latin. The first capital letter of the left-hand page had a woman's head with a snake's body copied on it, sitting on the bar of the letter 'A' like a swing. She was wearing a hat and a blue jacket-thing with gold stars painted on it. Her green-and-brown's snake's end fell below the bottom of the letter. On the facing page was a dragon, but white and with saucer-plate eyes. He looked a very young dragon and strangely out of place—but appealing somehow.

'It's Mrs Morgan,' Maddy laughed, pointing at the snake-woman. But her joke fell flat.

'What kind of a book is it, Uncle Alistair?' asked Ralph.

'It's trouble,' said Uncle Alistair grimly.

'Pardon?' queried Maddy, standing on tip-toe to have a better look at the book.

'This is a book of spells,' said Uncle Alistair. 'I can't think how it came to be among these others.'

Maddy laughed, but Ralph tensed a little and looked concerned.

'It doesn't say spells,' she said. 'It says "lore and superstition" here.' She looked up at Uncle Alistair. 'Oh, come on, nobody believes in spells.'

'The people who wrote that book did,' said Uncle Alistair.

'But that was long ago!' protested Maddy. 'This is now!'

But Uncle Alistair was far away, looking hard at the Latin letters and saying the words under his breath.

'Now isn't so different from then,' he said suddenly. 'We may have cars and electricity and televisions, but underneath all that people are still the same. The funny thing is that human beings are continually surprised to discover that they *are* the same. I suppose that's because most people spend a great deal of their lives trying to think that they're different.'

'Different?' asked Maddy.

'Oh, different from their parents, from their neighbours, from their friends at school. We always look at our differences because that's what makes us special. We don't look at the deep sameness that holds us all together, the deep sameness that's always been there.'

'But what were the monks doing with spells?' asked Ralph, his mind flipping back to the book in front of them.

'What indeed?' murmured Uncle Alistair. 'The monks collected knowledge where they could find it and wrote it down in books. They were writers as well as librarians: they had to be because no one else had the time or the skill to store knowledge. No doubt some of the monks followed their curiosity into dark places and learned secrets that would have been best forgotten. Spells can never be good. They can take you into a black country it's hard to escape from. But the monks felt they had to collect knowledge and they sometimes lost sight of what that knowledge was. And then—there are always some people who are hungry for power, and what surer way to gain power over someone than to cast a spell on them?'

'But you don't believe in spells, surely?' spluttered Maddy aghast. 'I mean, that's just for stories, isn't it?'

'Some stories are true,' answered Uncle Alistair, 'and others can come true. But we ought to go now.'

'It's time,' announced a voice from the door. It was the curator.

'I let you have five extra minutes,' he said. 'You can always come back tomorrow. We're open all day.'

'Thank you,' said Uncle Alistair. 'I think we will.' He cast a glance at Ralph and Maddy, who nodded vigorously. They hurried downstairs and stood for a few moments on the stone steps in the failing light. The windows of the buildings around them were yellow, warm and inviting. Curtains were being drawn and blinds let down. The cars already had their headlights on.

'It's too late for an ice-cream now,' shivered Uncle Alistair. 'I think we should go home—and you should go home, Maddy. Your mother will begin to worry. We'll walk that way.'

'Brr!' Maddy and Ralph hunched up their shoulders and walked with their hands deep in their pockets.

They crossed the road and turned right this time, away from the river, to zig-zag the quiet streets home. Cars passed. It was darker already, even since they had come out of the museum. Maddy glanced back at the statue of the king, a triumphant defender of the town in days long gone by. Suddenly she grabbed Uncle Alistair's arm. 'There! Did you see?' she hissed in alarm.

'What?' asked Ralph, sniffing and wiping his nose.

'There—behind one of the pillars outside the Tourist Information Office! Mrs Morgan! I'm sure I saw her!'

'Well, she is allowed to be there,' said Uncle Alistair, trying to soothe and defuse Maddy's worry.

'I suppose she is,' agreed Maddy, slackening her grip and putting her chilled hand back into her pocket. 'It's just—well, all that talk of spells. It made me feel—odd—that's all.' She smiled, and Ralph nudged her with one of his shoulders as a way of telling her not to be so stupid.

Uncle Alistair rubbed his eagle nose with his left hand and took a quick look behind him. So, Mrs Morgan. By the museum. Somehow he wasn't surprised. His eyes searched through the gloom back to the now-distant pillars. Maybe Maddy had seen her. Maybe she hadn't. Common sense told him that it was not important, but another, deeper sense told him that it was. Whatever the case, Uncle Alistair noted that Mrs Morgan wasn't there now.

3

It was a dream.

Or was it?

Uncle Alistair was lying in bed, the sheets pulled up to his chin. The curtains were open and the moonlight shone bright on his face. He didn't move. Ralph could see the headboard of his bed, the table standing beside it on its rickety legs, and the lamp switched off.

Uncle Alistair snored slightly in his sleep and was about to turn over—when—there was a mangled hiss and in through the window jumped a black cat. Its furry back arched up in an angry hoop and green fire glittered in its eyes. It was mewing and sneering. Placing its paws as cautiously as a ballet dancer on a tightrope, the cat walked from the window-sill onto the bedside table and sat down on Uncle Alistair's face.

For a moment nothing happened—the cat just sat there. Then Uncle Alistair began to thresh his body in panic and kick his legs. He clenched his fists under the blankets and struggled. But it was no use. It was no use at all—for the cat was growing heavier and heavier, larger and larger, like a ball of soot, like a weight, like a Big Black Thing until . . .

Ralph woke with a start and sat up in bed. He was alert and shivering. It had been a dream, only a dream, but a very real one. Much realler than the dreams he usually had. He padded out of bed and pulled back the curtains from his bedroom window. His room looked out over the back garden, fast asleep in the glimmer of the moonlight. There *was* a moon, then. But the roses were tucked up for the night and nothing outside stirred. Not even in Mrs Morgan's house.

Ralph turned and snuggled back into bed, pulling the blankets right up to his ears. He heard the slow creak of floorboards as Uncle Alistair crept through the night to the bathroom. He was awake too, then. Ralph wondered if his uncle had also had a dream. Maybe. But those were thoughts of the night when the mind is sharp and different and seems to follow other rules. Ralph knew that in the morning he wouldn't even mention it.

And he didn't. He must have fallen asleep again. There was sun streaming in through the window where the curtain was pulled back, making a long gold oblong on Ralph's bedroom carpet. The carpet was covered in train books, crayons, crushed-up paper—and clothes. Ralph got down on his hands and knees in his stripy pyjamas to gather up the clothes, shivered, and headed for the bathroom.

'When's Maddy coming round this morning?' asked Uncle Alistair. He was pouring dry muesli into two bowls, and an unopened pint of milk with a silver top was standing on the kitchen table. The radio was set to Radio 2, Ralph's mother's favourite station, and Uncle Alistair had not bothered to change it to Radio 4, which was always what *he* listened to.

'Tea? Coffee?' Uncle Alistair opened one of the cupboards on the wall to the left of the cooker and frowned.

'Tea,' said Ralph, 'I think.'

'You think?' echoed Uncle Alistair teasingly. 'Well, that's good news anyway. Did you sleep well?'

'Quite well.'

'I see—you think, and you slept quite well. I suppose

that's better than thinking badly and not sleeping at all. Hurry up and eat your muesli and I'll put on some toast—if there's any bread left. We might have to go to the shops today after all.'

Ralph sucked his spoon and kept quiet. The memory of the dream he had had pricked and worried him, but with Radio 2 filling the kitchen and Uncle Alistair's mind set firmly on where his mother had left the bread, Ralph didn't feel that it was the time to ask.

They were just washing up—Uncle Alistair washing, Ralph drying and putting away because he knew where everything went—when the doorbell rang.

'Maddy,' he said. He wiped his hands and went downstairs to the hall to pull back the bolt. Maddy stood at the door in her navy quilted anorak and white trainers.

'It's cold again today,' she said. 'Hello.'

'Do you want anything to eat?' asked Uncle Alistair, yelling down from the kitchen.

'I've just had breakfast!' returned Maddy, as loudly as she could, so that her voice would travel up the stairs.

'Then don't take your anorak off. I'll be right there.' Uncle Alistair emerged from the kitchen and hurried to his room with long, silent strides.

'What're we going to do today?' asked Maddy.

'The museum,' replied Ralph, half under his breath, for he already felt like a conspirator deep in some mysterious and sinister plot. 'We've got to go back and look at that book of spells. I think Uncle Alistair wants to persuade the man to take it out of its glass case.'

'Why?' asked Maddy, standing on one leg to see if she could balance properly.

'To see if he can read the spells,' retorted Ralph firmly. 'I think he thinks there's something important in that book.'

But Maddy just tutted and turned a pirouette.

'There,' exclaimed Uncle Alistair, running down the stairs. 'Are you ready, Ralph? We don't want to be too

29

late. We've got the lunch to get.' Uncle Alistair lifted his long trench coat off one of the pegs in the hall and did up the belt.

'We need some more milk, Ralph,' said his uncle. 'You won't forget to remind me, will you?'

It was less blowy outside than it had been the day before, but there was more cloud spread out like grey butter in the sky, and the pavement under their feet was damp and miserable. It was the sort of morning when you never know if you will need an umbrella or not. The three of them stepped off the narrow pavement to let a woman with a buggy pass, went in under the stone arch that led to the cathedral close, passing the glistening greystone giant of a building, and arrived at the High Street.

'Oh, look!' Ralph said, pointing puzzledly to something happening way down the road outside the museum.

'What's going on?' asked Maddy, screwing up her face.

Uncle Alistair, taller than most, and straighter, stared and for a moment said nothing. The main street where they were standing was barred to traffic, and clogged with people doing their shopping. Bikers sat on the steps of the dry fountain, and a tramp in a dirty brown coat tied with string was playing the mouth organ and holding out his cap for pennies. Outside the museum were two police cars with flashing lights, and cones had been put out so that no one could park.

'Come on,' ordered Uncle Alistair sternly, 'we must go and see.' He took Ralph's arm and Maddy's hand, one on each side of him, and all but dragged them down the street, moving so swiftly that the other people had to get out of his way. 'So rude!' remarked one woman as she smoothed down her coat. But Uncle Alistair didn't hear her or at least pretended not to. His eyes were fixed on the blue flashing lights, his mind trying to guess what they meant. At the museum steps a policeman blocked the doorway. 'I'm sorry, sir,' he said, 'but no one's allowed inside.'

'What—what's happened?' asked Uncle Alistair breathlessly.

'I'm afraid I'm not at liberty to say anything just yet,' answered the policeman. 'Now, if you'd care to move along...' Uncle Alistair stepped back and then caught sight of the curator lighting his pipe in the doorway.

'Halloo!' he called, waving. The curator adjusted his glasses and looked out. 'Oh, it's you,' he said. 'I suppose you've heard.'

'We haven't heard anything at all!' fumed Uncle Alistair, helpless with impatience. 'What's happened?'

'It'll be in all the papers,' said the curator glumly.

'Yes, but what?' asked Uncle Alistair again, more insistently this time.

'That book's been stolen. You know—the one in the middle in the glass case. The big one. There's going to be such a stink. The London people weren't keen on us having the exhibition in the first place. Not enough security they said. This isn't London, I said. Nothing much happens here. But it has. Swiped! Gone!' The man's eyes looked mournful and a little dewy behind his thick spectacles.

'I *am* sorry,' sympathized Uncle Alistair. 'Any idea who did it?'

'No,' answered the curator, his pipe trembling in his right hand. 'There was a burglar alarm, but it didn't go off. Funny that. No, there's a lot of people would give their eye teeth to get their hands on this lot. Dealers and such like. International. America. Who knows?'

'Who indeed. But they only took one book?'

'Yes, and it wasn't the most valuable. That's the queer thing. It was only that spell book, magic thing, that they wanted. I don't know—maybe someone collects them.'

'Obviously they do—or wanted that one, anyway. Well, we must leave you to it, but we'll come back again

31

after things have quietened down.'

'Do, but I don't think the books will be here. They'll probably be shipped off to London double quick now. There are a lot of people not very happy with me today. Goodbye!'

'Poor man!' said Uncle Alistair when the curator had gone.

'What, was that book stolen?' asked Maddy in some alarm.

'I'm sure it's nothing to get upset about,' said Uncle Alistair, steering Ralph and Maddy away. 'Just thieves.'

'Or *a* thief!' said Ralph grimly. He had his own thoughts on the subject.

'Or *a* thief!' agreed Uncle Alistair, with a cheerless laugh. 'Now, come on, we have some lunch to buy!'

'What do you think happened?' asked Maddy. Uncle Alistair had his arms full with a loaf and two pints of milk, while Ralph's pockets were weighed down with two large tins of baked beans.

'I really don't know,' Uncle Alistair replied. 'Anything can happen.'

'What if someone wants to cast a spell?' suggested Ralph with some concern. 'I mean, no one can stop them. No one would know,' and he looked aghast.

'We would know,' said Uncle Alistair, and he smiled. 'If someone does want to cast a spell out of that book, there is nothing we can do to stop them—at least—not yet!'

'Yet?' questioned Maddy quickly.

'Before you look for the cure you must find the illness,' said Uncle Alistair mysteriously. And he left it at that. 'Are you going home for lunch, or staying?'

'Staying, if that's all right,' said Maddy.

'Then I'll give your mother a ring at work.'

By now they were walking back along the road to where Ralph lived. The trees were dripping onto the parked cars and there was no one to be seen in any of the gardens. It was too wet. As they turned the corner into Ralph's street they caught sight of the postman standing outside Mrs Morgan's house. He had a package in his hand and was looking slightly puzzled.

'Anything wrong?' called Uncle Alistair, as they came near. The postman looked round. His van engine was still running. 'I have a parcel here for a Mrs Vivien Morgan,' he said, 'but I don't know anyone of that name—and there's no one in at this address. Do you live round here?'

'Oh, Mrs Morgan lives there right enough,' Ralph chipped in. 'She's new. She's only been in the house for a couple of weeks.'

'Hmm,' said the postman. 'Well, I suppose I'd better leave her a card and take this back to the sorting office.'

'Are you sure she's not in?' pressed Ralph. 'She never seems to go out—at least, not during the day.' As he said it, he suddenly realised just what he was saying.

'I have tried,' protested the postman, 'but I reckon I could try again.' He gave a heavy sigh. 'Hold this for a minute.' Uncle Alistair took the package, passing the milk and bread to Ralph. The postman took a notebook out of his pocket and scribbled something in it.

The package was covered in brown paper and tied up with string. As Uncle Alistair gazed at the handwriting he saw MRS VIVIEN MORGAN in swirling black letters, slightly smudged on the paper. In a split moment, as he continued to gaze, the letters seemed to curl, like seaweed or inky snakes, looping and twisting till they arranged and folded themselves into a different name altogether, a very black name, a name that Uncle Alistair had seen only once before, a very long time ago. Sweat broke out in tiny droplets on his forehead, and he wiped it away with the back of his left hand.

From Mrs Morgan's hedge above them, came a sudden hiss. All four started at the unexpectedness of the noise and looked up. 'Well, I'll be . . .' said the postman. It was a cat. A black cat with green eyes and white, stiff whiskers. It eyed them warily, angrily even—then seemed to sneer, turning its head this way and that. With one light bound it vanished, clean over the hedge, and into Mrs Morgan's garden.

The postman took back the parcel, pushed open the wrought-iron swing gate and walked carefully up the stone path. He pulled the bell and knocked loudly at the green door. There was silence. He knocked again, louder this time, and then, inside, a light clicked on. The door opened with a squeak and Mrs Morgan stood there. She looked commanding, with crow black hair pulled tightly behind her head and a neat black dress that came below her knees. She had a brooch of silver, in the shape of a magical five-pointed star, pinned to her left shoulder, and red lipstick drawn in a tight line over her lips. She was a small woman, dumpy even, but there was something about her that was alert and aware. It was as though she had eyes in every part of her body and knew how to see out of them.

'What do you want?' she snapped.

'Package for you, ma'am,' replied the postman. 'Will you sign for it?' She grabbed the postman's pen and made her mark on his clipboard—then took the package from him with an impatient tug. It was strange, but as she glanced down the path and caught sight of Uncle Alistair standing by the gate she seemed to jump a little. At least, that's what it looked like, but Ralph couldn't be sure. 'Thank you,' she said brusquely, and closed the door in one firm swift movement.

The postman hurried back down the path. 'Funny woman,' he muttered. 'Still, I suppose it takes all sorts. I'd better be on my way.'

'We had, too,' said Uncle Alistair.

'Time's wearing on,' shouted the postman. He waved

as he passed them in his van.

'I dare say it is,' said Uncle Alistair.

The three of them walked on to Ralph's house. As they stood on the doorstep, waiting for Uncle Alistair to find his key, none of them saw the bedroom curtains of Mrs Morgan's house part and a pair of keen green eyes gaze at them until they had disappeared inside.

4

As the evening drew on, the rustle in the trees seemed to quieten and still. The cloud above thickened and deepened and knotted in the sky, pressing down on the helpless, waiting land. The cloud first blotted out the sun and, later, the moon and the stars. A hush fell on the few people who ventured to walk the streets, for something was in the air. A prickle ran down the backs of their necks. Then, after a breathless long-drawn-out pause, it happened.

Far away, where the edge of the heavy cloud scraped the ridge of hills, the hills Ralph could see from his living-room window, there was a flash of white, bright light. It was answered after a few moments by a deep, echoing rumble that built up to a loud bang and then died away. It was like a firework, it was like a bomb, it was like—like a dragon wakening up after a long sleep.

It happened again.

Nearer it came. And nearer. Another long pause while the trees in the road waited, then a flash. The rumble came quicker this time. And quicker the next. But still there was no rain, just a stillness and a waiting outside.

Suddenly, Ralph saw it—a jagged sword of lightning that joined the cloud to the earth, and an angry, growling bellow of thunder that came right on top of it. It woke anything that could have been asleep in the night and challenged it with its power.

Then, mercifully, as if the night were sighing with relief, a patter of thick, heavy drops of rain began to fall, wetting the road, wetting the cars, wetting the houses and wetting the cricket field. Another flash and rumble and the rain was splattering in the drainpipes, gushing in brown foamy streams along the gutters, and swelling the river till it was dangerously near the brim of its banks.

'Bed,' said Uncle Alistair, folding his newspaper and switching off the television. The picture shrank to a solitary, fading dot. But, after he had put on clean pyjamas, with the mint taste of toothpaste still in his mouth, Ralph sat on the chair in his bedroom, elbows on the window-sill and watched the spectacle outside. The curtain of rain pounded the ground as if each drop were a nail. It obscured the night.

Who knew what might be going on—somewhere? Who knew what might be happening? It was a night to get up to things, secret things—when other people's minds were occupied elsewhere—if you knew what you were about.

Ralph crawled back into bed and rolled over onto his side to sleep. He left the curtains open and watched as the roofs of the flats and houses lit up moment after moment. He listened to the steady pour of the rain. And then . . . after a while . . . he fell asleep.

It was a bad night and news of some of the damage found its way into the local newspaper. The wind took some trees down just outside town near the motorway. And a farmer at Salem had to move up to the second floor of his house because of flooding from the river. The chimney fell off one house in Woodacre Avenue and narrowly missed a policeman hurrying home from the station. At Fitzknowe, a village not five miles away, the old oak tree in the marketplace burst into flames and toppled, crushing a telephone box. The tree was hundreds of years old, they said, and marked the spot where they used to burn witches. Maybe they were having their revenge now, suggested a few. What, after all this time, others said? And laughed. There weren't any witches now. That was just old tales. But the tree was down, right enough, and the story made the front page of the *Gazette*, with even the bit about witches in it.

Maddy lived with her mother in a small, modern flat in Queen's Gate Street, two streets away from where Ralph lived in Woodacre Avenue. Maddy's mother was older than Ralph's parents. Maybe not much older, but she *seemed* older. And Maddy's father was somewhere else. He had gone before Maddy could really remember, and so only faint glimpses of him remained in her head. At Christmas. One birthday. A boat trip when she was very small. And now she was alone with her mother who did not have very much money. And they lived in a flat.

Maddy's mother worked part-time for a lawyer, and, if Maddy's father had gone before she could really remember, Maddy's mother had worked at the lawyer's office for as long as she could remember. In fact, it seemed that all Maddy's life things had been the same—so much the same that she never ever thought they could be any different. Maddy's mother was kind, but kept herself to herself and never said very much. She was not at all like Ralph's parents, especially Ralph's mother, who would bang the piano and sing loudly when she was in the mood, and drag Maddy and Ralph off on special outings when the weather was fine. Housework didn't matter at all to Ralph's mother, but to Maddy's mother a clean house meant *everything*.

'I've run out,' announced Maddy's mother at breakfast, after the storm.

'What of?' asked Maddy, shaking the last of the cornflakes out of their cardboard packet into her bowl.

'Cornflakes for one thing, and Ajax for another. If I make up a little list, will you go and get the things for me? I have to be at the office early today.'

'No problem,' said Maddy, trying to pick out the bits of cornflakes that had mashed and stuck between her teeth. 'I'll go—I'm going round to Ralph's again this morning.'

'Well, try not to get in his mother's way. I'm sure she has more than enough to do with her own three children, without you as well.'

'She's not there,' said Maddy, taking a big slurp of tea. 'I thought I'd told you. She's gone away.'

'So who is there?' Maddy's mother began to show a little more interest than usual. She was intent on prising the top off her yolky soft-boiled egg with a knife.

'Ralph's uncle—his Uncle Alistair. He's very—strange—but quite nice.'

'Hmm,' said Maddy's mother. 'I can't see a man being much use about the place.'

'Oh, he's a lot of use,' chipped in Maddy. 'At least, I think he is. Only, I'm not sure *what* use. But we're going to find the book anyway.'

'What book?'

'The one that's been stolen from the museum.'

'Oh, *that* book. I did hear something. Good luck to you. But I hope this man isn't filling your head with nonsense, is he?' Maddy's mother looked sharp all of a sudden, and she flicked her napkin irritably. 'I've had enough nonsense in the past. Now, hurry back, mind,' and she gave Maddy a light kiss on the cheek.

The streets were wet and shiny after the storm, but quiet and peaceful. The whole town felt like a patient on a hospital bed recovering from an operation—peaceful, but bewildered. And there was still something hanging in the air that had not been cleared away.

'Terrible night,' Maddy heard one woman with a bag full of shopping say to a young woman wearing a yellow plastic sou'wester who was holding a toddler firmly by the wrist.

'Wasn't it?' she replied. 'I thought the whole house was

39

going to come down on top of me.' They laughed.

Maddy went to the Co-op and picked out the things her mother wanted. Most people still seemed to be talking about the storm or complaining about the rise in the price of tea and butter.

'Not that I'd have butter in the house,' declared one woman. 'It's not good for you. But Len won't have anything else.'

Maddy smiled as she joined the queue at the checkout. She loaded the three or four items she had bought into a plastic carrier bag and decided to cut home through the cathedral close.

The cathedral brooded over the town—silent and strong—as it had done for a thousand years or more. Maddy glanced at the great wooden door. She had been inside once or twice before Uncle Alistair's visit. Once on a school trip. Once with her grandmother—but not more than that. It was funny, she thought, how many hundreds of tourists arrived each year in gleaming coaches to tramp round the worn cathedral flagstones and gaze up at the stained glass windows. Yet the people who lived close by hardly ever went inside at all. What had Uncle Alistair meant, that there was more to cathedrals than stones and statues and organs? Was there something important, something under her very nose, that she had been missing all this while? She walked on, still thoughtful, swinging her plastic bag round on to the other hand.

'Did you hear it?' cried Ralph excitedly.

'I think everybody heard it,' replied Uncle Alistair, fiddling with the radio. 'It was louder than a football crowd in an avalanche.'

' ... And damage reports are still coming through. One intriguing incident is the fall of the great oak at Fitzknowe, the scene of witchcraft and dark doings in the seventeenth century. While many trees were brought down by the wind that rose at about three this morning, the oak at Fitzknowe appears to be the only casualty of the lightning itself. And now back to Geoff in the studio . . .' 'Thank you, Ron, and, to cheer up all you wet people out there— "Raindrops keep falling on my head" . . .'

'I think I'll find something else,' grunted Uncle Alistair. 'I suppose that was local radio. Hmm. I wonder what the dark doings *were*. Maybe we should try to find out.'

Then the phone rang, shrill and insistent from the hallway. *Brring brring. Brring brring.* 'You try and find something, Ralph. I'll go and see who that is.'

Uncle Alistair picked up the phone. It was Ralph's mother. 'Valerie—oh, hello. Yes, we're all fine here. How are you? It *is* a bad line, isn't it? It must have been the storm. Haven't you heard? It was terrible here last night. Nothing where you are? Well, that's lucky. How's . . . oh, she's better? That's good. But you know what she's like— always putting a brave face on everything. Ralph? Oh, he's fine. Yes, he's behaving himself—I am too, so far. What do you mean? I'm always good. Most of the time. Listen, do you happen to know anything about Fitz-knowe? Something about an oak tree? Yes? Well, it's fallen down. I mean, struck by lightning. What? What's that? Witches? Where would I find out more? The library—oh, the library at Marchbury House. Now, there's a thought. Yes, OK. Do you want a word with Ralph? Fine. Well, nice to hear from you. Here's Ralph. I'll go and be a good uncle and make him some breakfast . . .'

'Marchbury House,' murmured Uncle Alistair to himself. 'Hmmm . . .'

By the time Ralph had finished on the phone, Uncle Alistair had made a pot of tea and was browning two slices of toast under the grill.

'She says I've got to look after *you*,' smirked

Ralph defiantly.

'And maybe she's right at that,' replied Uncle Alistair. 'After all, she should know.'

Maddy turned left down what remained of the cathedral cloisters. They made a narrow path into the close. The close itself, which hugged against the cathedral, consisted of an arrangement of fine-looking houses and the choir school, grouped round a square of green turf with an apple tree growing in one corner. The apple tree seemed to have survived the storm well enough, though it was looking a little battered.

Maddy's gaze was drawn to a knot of people gathered round an ambulance parked outside the bishop's house. Its light was flashing and there was a noise of worried talk. She walked down the stone path that skirted the edge of the green and joined the little group.

'Poor man,' said one woman. 'His housekeeper found him this morning, as stiff as a board.'

'Is he dead, then?' shouted a deaf old man, who was leaning on a stick.

'Oh, no!' said the woman. 'They don't know what's wrong. Here he comes now.' Two ambulance men in uniform were carrying the bishop out of his house on a stretcher. There was a blanket over him, folded up to his chin. The crowd parted to let the men through and Maddy caught a glimpse of the bishop's face. It was yellow and papery, and his eyes were stary and empty. He wasn't moving at all. Not even an inch. In fact, he was just like a block of wood. The men loaded the bishop into the back of the ambulance and slammed the doors shut.

'Excuse me,' said Maddy, pushing her way through the bags and sticks and elbows and coats. Her home in Queen's Gate Street was on the other side of the close and she needed to pass by. But, as she squeezed past the railings outside the bishop's house, something odd caught her eye. There, daubed on the pavement in yellow paint and slowly dissolving in the wet, were some letters or signs. They had run into little rivulets and were disappearing fast—but there was something about them.

Maddy's gut tightened all of a sudden and she felt uneasy. Those letters felt—well, they somehow felt like Mrs Morgan. What could it mean? Maddy glanced furtively round. The crowd were nodding earnestly to one another and beginning to disperse as the ambulance splashed away. There was nothing to wait for now. The action was over. People trampled on the letters, walking this way and that, blurring them even more on the pavement. Maddy didn't have a pen or pencil with her. She could only try hard to memorize the uncanny signs as, slowly, they vanished, melting and sliding, dissolving into the wet . . .

'They were like this,' Maddy explained to Uncle Alistair a little later, sketching out one or two on the paper spread in front of her on the kitchen table.

'I see,' said Uncle Alistair softly, pressing the tips of his fingers together beneath his chin.

'But they were almost gone by the time I got there and people were walking all over them.'

'Nevertheless, they *were* there—or something was there. Of course, it could mean nothing at all, and probably doesn't . . . but . . .'

'But what?' interrupted Ralph, impatient to hear what his uncle was going to say. 'Did they have something to do with the bishop being ill?'

'I think maybe we need to do some detective work.'

'About what?' asked Maddy, puzzled.

'About that book for one thing, and about witches for another.'

'Oh, not witches again!' protested Maddy. 'I think it's all stupid.'

'But I presume you are going to come with us.'

'Oh, YES,' affirmed Maddy, her cheeks burning and turning her face fully towards Uncle Alistair. 'I'm not going to miss anything—if there is anything, of course.'

'Where shall we ask?' said Ralph.

'I need to find out how to get to Marchbury House first,' said Uncle Alistair. 'Do either of you two know?'

Ralph and Maddy shook their heads.

'It's not been open long,' said Maddy.

'In that case we should begin at the Tourist Information Office, and perhaps call on our friend the curator, at the museum.'

'OK,' agreed Ralph, sliding off his chair and letting his bare feet touch the floor. 'Let's go.'

'Keener and keener,' chuckled Uncle Alistair. And for a moment Ralph wondered if Uncle Alistair was just making everything up to amuse them because it was the holidays. You never knew with him, really you didn't.

As they reached the centre of town, they noticed that the atmosphere in the High Street was—well, *different* from usual. How, it was hard to explain. People were going about their business as normal, but there was a strange heaviness in the air that was new and odd. Perhaps it was something to do with the storm. People were still talking about that and how strange they had felt when they had got up that morning. Still, it wasn't just that. There were—little things. Odd things. More people sitting down on the benches than usual, for one thing. And they weren't talking to each other: that *was* unusual. Just sitting and staring into space, with bags of shopping at their feet. Just sitting, even though the street was wet and shiny and it was cold.

Ralph shivered.

Then there was a business man sitting on the steps of the fountain were the bikers gathered. Just sitting with his briefcase and rolled umbrella between his knees, and wiping his forehead. You could tell he was anxious. You could see it in his face. As though he felt ... threatened. Threat. Threat. Yes, that was it. That was the word that somehow made everything fit into place. But how? Or why?

Ralph paused for a moment outside the windows of Marks and Spencers. Then there was a cry and gasp, as the people beside him surged forward. A woman had collapsed on the pavement. Tomatoes rolled out of her bag onto the wet, tarry road. Somebody stepped on one, squashing it with the heel of her shoe.

It was Mrs Morgan.

Ralph froze and said nothing. He watched as she disappeared into the crowd. A man, meanwhile, had pressed the fainting woman's head between her knees, fanned her, and brought her round. Two or three others were helping her to her feet, and a woman with two children was picking up her shopping. Uncle Alistair nodded at Ralph and they moved back through the crowd. Ralph noticed his uncle's frown.

'What's down this street?' he asked.

'The town hall,' said Ralph. 'Do you want to go and have a look?'

'I think we'd better,' suggested Uncle Alistair. 'Do you see what's going on over there?'

Ralph peered round the corner of the street at the massive Victorian gothic town hall. An eyesore, most people called it: like a dungeon and a wedding cake all in one. Parked in front of it on the double yellow lines was an ambulance with a blue flashing light.

Maddy ran up, breathless. 'Have you seen?' she asked. Uncle Alistair nodded but said nothing. Without a sound he bounded down the street to where the crowd of people had gathered. A policeman appeared and murmured into his walkie-talkie. Ralph and Maddy ran up behind Uncle

45

Alistair, in time to see two stretchers being carried out of the building.

'Food poisoning!' whispered Uncle Alistair into Ralph's ear. 'At least, that's what the cleaner says.' He pointed out a woman in an overall who was crying.

'She found them,' added Uncle Alistair by way of an explanation.

'Who are they?' hissed Maddy, standing on tip-toe and whispering in Uncle Alistair's ear.

'The mayor and his secretary,' answered Uncle Alistair.

'What! The mayor *and* the bishop, both in one day!' exclaimed Ralph in a disbelieving voice. 'What *is* going on?'

'Both in one day,' echoed Uncle Alistair seriously. 'And that's not all. Look down there!'

Dribbling and dissolving under the feet of the bystanders, yet unmistakable, were the remains of some markings splashed on the pavement in yellow paint.

'I think we've seen enough,' said Uncle Alistair. 'We should move on now.'

They halted outside the Tourist Information Office. 'Just wait here,' said Uncle Alistair, as he pushed open the plate-glass door. 'I'll only be a minute.'

Maddy and Ralph settled behind the pillars of the imposing building as Uncle Alistair talked to a balding, rather nervous man, inside. The man nodded furiously as Uncle Alistair spoke. He pointed to Marchbury House on a map on the wall with the tip of his blue biro pen.

'I'm cold,' complained Maddy.

'And hungry,' added Ralph.

'It's not been a nice morning,' she continued. 'It's not been a nice morning at all.'

Uncle Alistair pulled open the Tourist Information Office door and rejoined them. 'That seems simple enough,' he said, 'and we can walk there provided it doesn't come on to rain.'

'What about a bus?' asked Maddy.

'Oh, buses! You won't see anything from a bus. Buses are for people who want to go from A to B without a thought of how they're getting there. I like walking. And so will you. Come on.'

He led them across the road, dodging the cars, just by the statue of the king. The king was watching the town with an expression unchanged by the passing years.

'I wonder what *he* knows,' thought Ralph.

A lorry rumbled past them. A car sounded its horn. They crossed.

Their friend, the curator, was behind his till.

'Oh, it's you,' he said, blinking behind his spectacles. He took them off and rubbed the dusty lenses with a dirty handkerchief. 'I'm afraid they've closed the exhibition and taken all the books away. London and the Marchbury people are furious. With me, mainly.'

'I wanted to ask you something.' Uncle Alistair cleared his throat.

'Fire away!' invited the curator. He put his heavy glasses on again.

'I'm a historian—of sorts . . .' began Uncle Alistair.

'You didn't mention that before,' interrupted the curator.

'No, African antiquities is more my line,' continued Uncle Alistair. 'But I am a bit of the medievalist on the side and I've done some work on—spells and that sort of thing. It was the book of spells that was stolen, wasn't it?'

The curator grunted in agreement and blinked.

'Do you know anything about witches in these parts—in the past, of course?'

Uncle Alistair gave a little laugh, that sounded hollow and half-hearted. He was trying to persuade the curator he was less interested in the subject than he really was, but the curator wasn't taking much notice.

47

'Witches,' he muttered. 'That's a difficult one. I don't know much about that. There were the Frewin witches, of course, but they weren't medieval. Seventeenth century. It was only about that time, when people got religion in a big way, that they started to hunt down witches. Before that people would go to them for charms or medicines, or just leave them alone. Poor women. Old and alone— widows mostly. Though some of them may have been witches.'

'Yes, yes, I know,' said Uncle Alistair impatiently, butting in. 'But do you know any more than that—about local witches, I mean.'

'Hmm, I think you'll have to go up to Marchbury House for that,' deliberated the curator. He scratched his head. 'They've got a display up at the house about Lord Marchbury. A great one for witches, he was, in the seventeenth century. And there are still some books in the library there. I think so, anyway. I haven't been up there since they put on this new exhibition—and I'm scared to show my face at the moment. But go there. They're open in the afternoons.'

'Thank you,' said Uncle Alistair, 'I'll do that.' He gave a quick nod of gratitude to the curator and with one arm motioned Maddy and Ralph out of the building.

'I can do that this afternoon,' he murmured to himself, looking up at the sky. The cloud was now breaking in places and the streets were beginning to dry. Patches showed through the retreating wet.

'I can go on my own if you two want to do something else.'

'SOMETHING ELSE!' Ralph was aghast. 'No, we want to find out too. We'll come with you.'

Maddy agreed dumbly and fiddled with the cords of her hood. She looked a little unwilling, though.

They strolled back to Ralph's street, to be greeted by the loud roar of a dustcart and the shouts of men in orange.

'Oh, the dustmen!' cried Ralph. 'I forgot to tell you. We've got to put the rubbish out today. I'm sorry!'

Uncle Alistair tutted and gazed down at Ralph. 'Don't worry. There's still time. I'll nip ahead and do it,' and off he hurried, his long legs measuring well-spaced strides on the pavement.

'There's something funny about that uncle of yours,' said Maddy.

'I know,' said Ralph.

'No, I mean *really* funny,' insisted Maddy.

Uncle Alistair turned the key in the lock of Ralph's front door and disappeared inside. The dustmen were advancing slowing down the street: they still had three houses to go before they reached Ralph's. Ralph and Maddy idled, watching the source of the approaching din—the big dustcart with the iron masher in the back, that the men emptied the bins into. Then a thought struck Ralph.

There was a black plastic bin standing outside Mrs Morgan's house with all the others. They were in line, like silent soldiers, parading and guarding the street. Mrs Morgan's bin was right beside her gate, and the high hedge shielded her house from the road. Neither Ralph nor Maddy could possibly be seen from any of the windows.

'Do you think...' began Ralph. He gave Maddy a funny look.

'What?' asked Maddy.

'Let's have a look in here,' continued Ralph. He halted and cautiously lifted the lid off Mrs Morgan's dustbin. Both of them peered over the edge and looked inside. There, on top of the egg shells and potato peelings and torn cardboard packets and bashed tin cans, lay an empty tin of yellow paint and a brush.

'Wow!' exclaimed Ralph, open-mouthed, and slammed the lid on again quickly. But Maddy only bit her tongue and stared. She was really worried now.

5

Marchbury House stood a short walk out of town and half way up a hill. It was a large, square and imposing building with pillars and was situated at the end of a gravel drive behind two tall, stone gateposts capped by rampant lions. The house had first been built by Sir Percy Marchbury some time in the fifteenth century. But, as is the way with these places, it had been burned, rebuilt, extended and burned again as the years passed. The house had a wide view of the soft valley that fell away before it, and was crowded in by woods on the other three sides. The soft gravel glistened in the fresh rain that was now falling like a gauze over everything. An arriving clump of American tourists folded their umbrellas, exclaiming over everything, as they prepared to mount the steps and go inside. 'OPEN 2–5' declared a newly-painted notice. ADULTS £2.50. CHILDREN £1.50. TEAS.

'It's expensive,' remarked Maddy, shaking some drops from her hood and pushing back her hair.

'It's on me,' replied Uncle Alistair as he lowered his black umbrella like a shield. He took out his leather wallet and extracted a ten-pound note.

The house had not been open to the public for long, and there was still a lot of restoration to do. Scaffolding propped up one of the side walls and there was a cement mixer on the left of the path. The grass had run wild and was long and dripping in the rain. Moss grew through the cracks in the worn paving, and there were piles of sand and pebbles where work had started. Another sign, with an arrow attached, said PARKING.

Inside the main door there was a spacious hall, painted white, with a grand staircase leading up to the next storey. Just under this stair was a counter with leaflets laid out to tell you about the house. One cost 40p and the other, a glossy book, cost £3.50. THE EXHIBITION BEGINS HERE was fixed to the wall leading into one room on the right. A young man with a badge in his lapel was standing by it.

'Shall we ask him about what we've come for?' suggested Ralph.

'Hmm?' queried Uncle Alistair absentmindedly. 'Oh, no, I think we want our money's worth first, don't we? Let's see what they've got here—for £2.50.'

He put his umbrella into the stand under the coats and laid his gloves on the counter. He paid, took his change and came back to join them. 'He says it's very good,' said Uncle Alistair. 'And who knows, it might be!'

Neither Ralph nor Maddy liked big houses very much. Ralph's mother didn't either, so he hadn't visited many, but Maddy's mother did—and she had often been dragged to different stately homes and castles on a Sunday afternoon—bored.

Today, unfortunately, was no great exception. Because the house had not been opened for long, there was not much to show: the trustees were still trying to put the collection in order. The whole of the upstairs was closed for redecoration. It was possible, however, to go down into the cold, gloomy basement to look at the kitchen with its old ovens, and the wine and game cellars. There were only three rooms on the ground floor for the small number of visitors to wander round.

One room was full of paintings—mainly of the March-bury family, by Dutch and French minor artists. None of the paintings were very famous, and neither Maddy nor Ralph found any of them very interesting. There were men and women posing in old clothes, with dogs or children—and a few landscapes. The walls of the room were papered red and an electric glass chandelier hung down from the roof. Long, white net curtains billowed a little at each of the tall windows.

Maddy and Ralph completed a circuit of the whole room in a matter of minutes, but Uncle Alistair insisted on stopping in front of each painting and scrutinizing it carefully. He seemed to be labelling and recording each flake of paint in that strange mind of his. Then he would nod quietly to himself and move on to the next one.

The second room they entered was stocked with household implements of various kinds and from various centuries—knives and forks, vases and wash bowls, buckets and brooms and furniture—and some tailor's dummies draped in costumes of the fifteenth century. That was—well—not really *much* more interesting. Even Uncle Alistair did not stop long there.

And the third room showed a history of the house and family, with paintings, photographs and scale models. Ralph and Maddy took one look at all this and sloped off, muttering, to a window.

'I've had enough,' moaned Maddy.

'Me too,' said Ralph. 'There's nothing to do here. We should have let him come on his own.' Ralph swivelled round and, as he did so, his voice trailed away and the colour left his face. His eyes were fixed to something on the wall.

'What is it?' asked Maddy, seeing him freeze. 'Have you seen something?'

But Ralph had already wandered away to stand underneath an impressive picture in a gold gilt frame. Maddy followed, feeling unsure, and paused at Ralph's side. In the middle, a little to one side, three women were tied to wooden stakes with bonfires heaped around them. Obviously they were witches. On the right-hand side of the painting was a group of men in finer clothes and one, with a curly beard and soft, floppy hat was pointing at the women with a feather. He must have been using it as a pen, because he was holding up a roll of paper with something written on it in his other hand.

Ralph and Maddy scanned the canvas. The middle witch was different from the other two. They were old and bowed, screaming for mercy with pleading eyes. But she was young and proud, and had turned her face away from the accusing man. The painting, vivid and bold, showed her crow-black hair and fine features to good advantage. She was younger, certainly, but there was no mistaking it.

'Mrs Morgan!' gasped Maddy. 'It must be her! It must be! It must!' All at once, Maddy began to shake uncontrollably, and the tears ran down her cheeks. She sniffed, sobbing, and reached for her handkerchief.

Uncle Alistair noticed at once that something was wrong and came over to see. Ralph was ashen and worried.

'It's—it's—Mrs Morgan!' stammered Ralph, pointing at the painted woman with a disbelieving forefinger.

Uncle Alistair gazed at the picture with a satisfied expression. He examined every part of it. 'So,' was all he had to say. Then he broke off. 'Have you two got carried away?' he scolded gently, putting his arms round their shoulders. 'It can't possibly be Mrs Morgan. This picture was painted hundreds of years ago.'

'Well, maybe she's come back!' sniffed Maddy—so loudly that a woman's head turned at the other side of the room.

'Nonsense!' scoffed Uncle Alistair. 'People don't come back—unless they've never been away. Dry your tears and we'll ask the man what we came to find out.'

But Ralph was uneasy. He was disturbed by the picture and the proud young woman with her head turned away.

It was the one, the only, painting in the room without any description or history attached to it.

'Come now,' soothed Uncle Alistair. 'It's not what you think.'

He took them over to the man, who was now standing behind the counter. He was on the phone, and clearly not in the best of moods.

'I see,' he sighed. 'Terrible! Terrible! I suppose Wednesday will have to do then.' He slammed the receiver down with such a bang that the bell of the phone jangled. 'What *is* going on down there!' he exclaimed.

'I don't know what you mean,' said Uncle Alistair in his quiet, pleasant voice. It was the sort of voice that encouraged people to go on talking.

'Down in the town,' said the man. 'Everybody's either ill or not going out. It's ridiculous! First I hear on the radio that the bishop's gone as stiff as a board and nobody knows why. Then the mayor is carted off to hospital with food poisoning. And then, to crown everything, the chief constable collapses at a meeting—something to do with his heart.'

'The chief constable!' squealed Ralph.

'Yes! And now the builders say that they've got two men off sick and won't be able to do any more work upstairs until Wednesday. "Probably Wednesday"— which could mean any time next week. You know builders!'

'Sadly, yes,' sympathized Uncle Alistair. 'Builders of all kinds. But we,' and he indicated Maddy and Ralph along with himself, 'are not so much interested in builders as in books.'

'What kind of books?' The man suddenly halted in his flow.

'Well, we were wondering if we could see the library.'

'I'm afraid the library's closed at the moment for supposed decoration. All the books are under wraps.

Besides, *they*,' and he pointed at Maddy and Ralph with his pen, 'wouldn't be allowed in. So I'm afraid you'll have to wait a couple of months.'

'That *is* a pity,' said Uncle Alistair. 'You see, I *am* a historian, and I came specially to see the very interesting exhibition at the museum—the books from Melton Abbey. Only it seems that someone has stolen what was, for me, the most interesting of all the books—the book of spells.'

'You don't have to tell me!' The man threw up his hands in despair. 'If it's not one thing, it's another. We've had the police over every square inch of this place looking for clues, and the curator down there's been no help. Police and builders! No wonder the chief constable fell over with his heart!'

'No wonder he did!' Uncle Alistair looked a little rueful and dismayed. 'I'm sorry to waste your time—and to be so disappointed.'

'Come specially, you say,' muttered the man. 'Come specially all the way from London?'

'All the way,' repeated Uncle Alistair.

Ralph watched his uncle closely. Something seemed to be happening. As Uncle Alistair drew himself to his full height he appeared to be much taller than normal. And he—magnetized—somehow. Ralph felt his uncle's presence expand and fill the hall, like scent or a piece of background music. You would, perhaps, have noticed it if it had been pointed out; you would certainly have noticed it once it had vanished. It was that kind of thing. The man's eyes were shining strangely and he could not take them away. 'Maybe I can help you,' he said, in a soft, pliant voice.

'Oh, I am glad,' said Uncle Alistair.

'You see, we did take some photographs of that book, and copied those, though they aren't too clear.'

'It would be nice to have a copy,' hinted Uncle Alistair.

'Then I can do what I came to do after all.'

'Yes,' agreed the man. He frowned, as though he were lost. He seemed to have woken up out of a dream and didn't quite know where he was. 'I'll—I'll go and see what I can do.' He walked off shakily to a door opposite the entry to the exhibition marked STAFF.

'What did you do to him?' asked Ralph, looking up at his uncle in an accusing way.

'I don't know what you mean,' retorted Uncle Alistair.

'Yes, you do. He wasn't going to say anything—and then he did. How did you do that?'

'Charm!' said Uncle Alistair. 'Nothing more and nothing less. Now, here he comes, so you'd better not break it.'

The man returned with an open manila envelope tucked under his arm. 'Here you are,' he announced vaguely. 'It's a copy, so you can keep it.'

'Oh, *thank* you,' said Uncle Alistair. He took the envelope firmly in his slender fingers. 'Now ...'

'The painting!' hissed Ralph suddenly. 'Don't forget the painting!'

'Oh, yes!' Maddy put her hand to her mouth.

Uncle Alistair cleared his throat. 'Can you—by any chance—tell us the history of—the—er—painting in the—er—third exhibition room. Is it associated with the house?'

'The witches, you mean?'

'Ah, yes,' said Uncle Alistair brightening, 'that's the one.'

'Let me see. It's a bit of a black episode in the history of this place.'

'Hmm,' nodded Uncle Alistair encouragingly, 'do go on.'

'The man in the painting is Sir Oliver Marchbury. He was a notorious witch hunter. The three women depicted are witches being burned in the marketplace in the town.

He's holding up their death warrant in one hand to show the power of the law and—oh—it was his idea actually to have an artist on the spot to sketch the scene. Now ... it's gone right out of my head. I can't think why. I'm sure I knew the whole thing off pat a couple of days ago. But I've got a leaflet somewhere—ah, here you are. It's in Latin— from the history of the house, with a brief explanation on the other side. That'll tell you all you need to know. Wait a minute—the Doomwitch! That's what she was called. The Doomwitch! I'm sure of it.'

A window banged and Ralph and Maddy jumped.

'Well, we'll be going now,' said Uncle Alistair. 'Thank you for all your help. You've been most kind.'

As they closed the main door of the house carefully behind them and set off down the path, the man rubbed his eyes for a moment as though he were dizzy and shook his head to clear the strange feeling he had.

'How funny,' he mumbled to himself. 'What was I doing? I must have dozed off or something. Now, where *was* I?'

Uncle Alistair, Maddy and Ralph scrunched along the gravel drive, cut across the main road, and followed the muddy path that led down to the river and back into town. But almost from the moment they left the house, they felt plunged into something—odd. A different atmosphere. Something in the air. The nearer and nearer they drew to the rows of houses that lay on the other side of the fields, the more Ralph experienced an uncomfortable tightening within him. It was a kind of alarm that he could not explain. And he did not want to. Instead, it pulled at him—it pulled at them all. Gradually, as they continued walking, their conversation crumbled into silence, and it became very difficult to start it up again.

At last, as they came to the bridge across the meadows, Maddy confessed, shaking: 'I'm frightened—don't you feel it?'

'Oh, yes,' agreed Uncle Alistair quietly, through his teeth. 'I feel it. I think everybody feels it. The threat is growing.' He hunched his shoulders and buried his right hand deep in his coat pocket. Fine drops of rain, so fine you could hardly see them, fell onto Uncle Alistair's umbrella. Underfoot the meadow was sodden, squashy and muddy, as though it were dissolving back into the earth. The grass soaked the bottoms of their jeans and trousers, and mud stuck to their shoes.

After a few more moments of silence they reached the gate at the end of Stanton Road. There was no one around. Maddy and Ralph clambered quickly over the bars, and Uncle Alistair undid the gate to let himself through. 'What a miserable day!' he said—and his words were like a judgement.

Maddy knotted the cords of her hood even tighter and wriggled her toes where her socks had got damp through her shoes. It was not a comfortable feeling. Strangely, instinctively, both Maddy and Ralph moved closer to Uncle Alistair as they walked along the empty street. They became more and more conscious of their own footsteps, the only noise they could hear apart from the soft fall of the rain. There didn't even seem to be any traffic.

Ralph looked up at the houses as they passed. Some of them had their curtains drawn, as though they were afraid to face the outside world. A dog snuffled in a dustbin, its coat stuck down on its back with the wet. In the distance were one or two people, out walking. Yet the *feeling* was that nothing stirred. That everyone was afraid. That everything was waiting. But for what?

Maddy's right foot splashed in the gutter. She *was* wet now. And, in the distance, a church clock pealed five.

'I ought to go home,' announced Maddy.

'Be careful,' said Uncle Alistair. 'Go straight home. Turn neither to the left, nor to the right.'

'But I've got to turn right to get into Queen's Gate Street!' spluttered Maddy, confused and bewildered.

'You know what I mean,' said Uncle Alistair, and, in a flash, she did. She hurried off, splashing in the puddles on the pavements—all pricked with the heavier rain that had started to fall. Ralph and Uncle Alistair watched till she became a speck in the distance.

'Will she be all right?' asked Ralph.

'I think so,' said Uncle Alistair. 'At least, today.'

He and Ralph walked on home. Inside, in the hall, they shook themselves like dogs.

The grandfather clock's ticking was more reassuring than ever, and louder somehow. And it was warm in the house with its familiar smells and furniture.

'It's a promise, you see,' pointed Uncle Alistair, rapping his knuckle on the glass where the rainbow was painted onto the clock face. You know the story: there was a promise to Noah and the animals that there would be no more floods, no more destruction. Everything will turn out all right. All shall be well, and all manner of things shall be well.'

'It keeps good time,' said Ralph, taking off his shoes and throwing them, one after the other, onto the newspaper.

'Ah, well, it's important to keep time if you can. Time is such a funny thing, you see. It goes forwards, but sometimes it goes backwards. You never know where you are with it. Now you can go and watch television—I have some translating to do.'

He tapped the rain-spattered manila envelope with the fingers of his left hand, as if he was drumming a tune on it.

Neither of them saw, far above them, on the roof of their house, sloping along the gutter, the black cat they had seen on top of Mrs Morgan's hedge. Its green eyes burned as it gave an angry hiss and tore a beaded cobweb from the drainpipe with its claw.

Maddy hurried home. She ran so fast that she got a stabbing stitch in her right side and had to slow down, scuffing her shoes on the pavement. There was hardly anyone around now at all. The light in Mr Shah's grocery was on, but the shop seemed empty. A few cars passed by, but not many. Every movement Maddy made was somehow like a struggle against something heavy—like wading through thick treacle. Even the cars, when they were moving, appeared to be moving very slowly. It was with some relief, therefore, that Maddy at last reached Queen's Gate Street and climbed the stairs to her flat. Home. She turned the key and went in.

'Is that you, dear?' called a weary voice.

'Yes!' shouted Maddy, taking off her shoes. She hung up her anorak and rubbed the drops out of her hair with a towel from the bathroom. 'Just coming!'

Maddy's mother was sitting in the living-room in the half-dark, with neither the television nor the lights on. She was propped up on the sofa and appeared to be tired to the point of being completely worn out.

'What's wrong?' asked Maddy, coming in via the kitchen with a glass of orange in her hand.

'I don't know,' sighed Maddy's mother. She closed her eyes for a moment as if in pain. 'It's been—such a funny day...' Then her voice slackened off to nothing.

'Tell me!' Maddy plumped herself down in the armchair at right angles to her mother, and perched nervously on the very edge. She gripped the glass she was holding and took a sip of the drink.

'Well...' Maddy's mother put her hand to her forehead. It was difficult for her to concentrate. So many things seemed to be slipping out of her mind, and all at once.

'Shall I call the doctor?'

'Doctor? Oh, no! Not a doctor. I'm not ill—just—tired. You see,' she adjusted her position and began to speak, 'when I got to work I found that Mr Matthews had been taken ill. Mr Matthews, the man I work for. And his wife was very upset on the phone because someone had splashed the pavement outside their house with yellow paint. Anyway, I got to work. There was quite a backlog—but—I don't know—everything I tried to do went wrong. All the people I phoned were either out or ill and—I know it sounds silly—but everything in the High Street just seemed to slow down—gradually. I can't explain it at all. Then I began to feel ill—heavy, sort of—and, well, frightened. And, you know, I'm sure everyone was feeling the same, though no one would admit it, of course. But I stayed on to the bitter end and came home.

'I've lived in this town for twenty years and walked that same road to and from work every day except weekends and holidays and never, never in all my born days have I been so scared. I was very nearly clean out of my wits. And the worst of it all was that I couldn't explain it. I don't know. Maybe I'm just getting ... old. Maybe it's the weather.' She smiled weakly at Maddy. 'Have you had a nice day?'

'All right,' said Maddy. 'Ralph's uncle took us up to Marchbury House.'

'How interesting,' approved Maddy's mother.

'Yes,' lied Maddy, 'it was.'

'I'm so glad Ralph has a *cultural* uncle. I feel much happier about that.'

'Oh, he knows all sorts of things,' replied Maddy.

'You know,' yawned Maddy's mother, sinking back again after a brief, momentary brightness, 'I've just realised what the feeling is—what I've got inside of me—what's hanging over everyone—what's stifling the town.'

'What is it?' asked Maddy, trembling a little and taking another slurp of the orange.

61

'It's the feeling of doom,' pronounced Maddy's mother, and she turned her face to the wall.

6

Now it was Maddy's turn. To have a dream. A dream. Tossing and turning in her bed she saw blackness, deep and utter and complete, without stars. Then, like a battered old coin, the moon came out to hang in the sky. But its light was feeble and fitful and did not penetrate far. Somewhere, suddenly, at the back of the dark, there was a yowl, and a black cat, Mrs Morgan's cat, leapt onto the lip of the moon. It balanced there, its green eyes filled with unearthly, fizzing sparks. It was holding the missing book of spells between its paws. With a turn of its head it lengthened its back and opened the book, pages downwards, over the abyss, and shook. It shook and shook and shook. Hard.

After a moment, little sparks began to tumble from the pages of the book, like stars or silvery flakes of snow. And, as the stars fell close to the sleeping earth, so they grew, swelling in size and roundness and brightness. At last, as though bursting from eggs, they turned into creatures— or Maddy saw that they had, in fact, been creatures all the time.

The dragon with saucer eyes was there, and the woman with the body of a snake. A silver leopard with mouldy green spots gave a bloodcurdling roar, and there was a wild boar, a bear, a deer with golden antlers, a cockatrice, a harpy, a host of dogs and cats of all shapes and sizes— and, last but definitely not least, a leviathan. The leviathan, a huge ungainly water monster, sloped down out of the book, its massive body coiling sluggishly to the ground while its tail was still pressed between the pages up on the edge of the moon.

Maddy was afraid and wondering—her face shone with the otherworldly light that filled and stunned the dark night . . . when, with a graceful bound out of nowhere came Ralph's Uncle Alistair. He put a finger to his lips to show Maddy to be quiet and, out of the inside of his jacket, he took an umbrella. It was almost invisible. 'Stand under here,' he whispered, 'and nothing will fall on you.' He put his arm round Maddy and held her close to him while, with a flick, he put up the umbrella. It was made of gossamer or spiders' webs and it shimmered and glimmered under the night sky.

And what he said was true. Nothing did fall on top of the umbrella, or, if it did, it vanished—bursting like a bubble and leaving only a mix and gauze of colours hanging in the air for a brief moment before there was nothing again. Yet, even though Maddy and Uncle Alistair were safe under the umbrella, the animals were still falling thick and fast around them. It really was raining cats and dogs. Maddy saw that the moment they touched the ground they seemed to spring into real, bodily life and went lumbering, jumping, running, crawling or slithering away into who-knows-where—somewhere in the heart of the night.

'Tch!' said Uncle Alistair. 'Let's see,' and, looking at Maddy, he tossed the umbrella up into the air.

'Oh, no!' cried Maddy, holding her arms out after it.

But up, up and up it went. Up flew the umbrella and, the moment the moon's rays touched it, it burst into a glory of rainbow colours—red and yellow and green and blue and indigo, and spread out like paint, like a bridge, all over the sky. Maddy watched, amazed, finding that she and Uncle Alistair were now standing snug under the rainbow. And what a rainbow! It was huge. Huger than Maddy had ever seen. And Ralph was there, and her mother, and Ralph's father and mother, and—oh, hundreds of others. They were all there, safe and sound, under the rainbow.

And as Maddy looked up at the moon, it began to shake and vibrate and ring. As though it were angry or frightened or having some kind of fit. And Maddy was suddenly worried for the moon that acted like a sobbing child. So she lifted up her hand, and her arm stretched and stretched. It stretched right up to the rim of the moon. And when it got there, she brushed off Mrs Morgan's cat like a dead fly. Then she took hold of the moon . . . to stop it ringing and shaking so. And she put her hand on it . . . and found . . . it was only her alarm clock. It said half-past eight.

'It was a dream,' thought Maddy, 'but how real!'—and she rolled back and over in the blankets.

Ralph's mother rang. 'I've been trying for ages,' she complained. 'is there something wrong with the phones down there?'

'There's something wrong with *everything* down here,' Ralph muttered into the receiver. He was still in his pyjamas, and his feet were cold and bare on the hall floor.

'Is my—crackle—brother there—crackle? There, it's doing it again.'

'I'll go and see. Uncle Alistair!' shouted Ralph.

Uncle Alistair had been up for a large part of the night with the copies of the spell book that the man at March-bury House had given him. He had been translating slowly from Latin, not a language he knew *very* well, until his eyes had hurt and gone bloodshot. So he was tired this morning and shadows had gathered under his eyes. Pale, he yawned, and stifled it with his hand.

'Who is it? My sister?' he asked, appearing from the bathroom. 'Good—oh, Valerie. Good morning. How are things?' he said, taking the receiver.

'I—crackle crackle—can't—crackle crackle—hear

you very well.'

'No, there appears to be some fault in the line and . . . Valerie, can you hear me? Valerie? Valerie?'

Uncle Alistair made a face and held the receiver upside down by the cord as though it were some kind of smelly, dead fish.

'We seem to have a problem,' he drawled, lifting his eyebrows at Ralph.

'What's the matter?' asked Ralph, tension clutching at his throat.

'The phone's dead,' said Uncle Alistair. 'Listen!'

Ralph took the phone and held it to his ear. There was nothing. Well, not a phone noise anyway—just a distant swaying, like the wind moaning between the telegraph wires.

'It's a bit of a nuisance,' Uncle Alistair said as he dialled 100 for the operator. Nothing. And then 192 for Directory Enquiries. Nothing. Just the distant swaying sound of the wind, murmuring something secret that neither of them could understand.

'What about Maddy's phone? We could use that. Downstairs is away—so Mr Patterson's phone is out.'

'I think,' replied Uncle Alistair in a clipped voice, 'that Maddy's phone and probably every other phone in the town is in exactly the same state as ours.'

Maddy pulled on her clothes and brushed her hair, squinting in the mirror all the while. It was funny, because her mother was usually up long before she was, and always hurrying her out of bed. But the flat was quiet and in half-darkness and all the curtains were still drawn. The washing-up hadn't been done from the night before and lay piled beside the sink, while the newspaper was in sheets on the living-room carpet. Maddy opened the curtains to a brighter day with a weak, watery sun. The rain had stopped, at least. She went into the bathroom and switched on the heating to take the edge off the morning chill in the flat. Quietly, and a little timidly, she knocked on her mother's bedroom door.

There was a moan from inside. 'Maddy, is that you?' It was her mother's voice, but weak and worn. Maddy put her head round the door. 'Are you all right?' she asked, trying to hold back the alarm that was rising in her voice.

'No, well—no, not really. I've been having such awful dreams. Such black, black dreams. But no. I've got no energy. None at all. It must be this bug that's going round the office.' She sighed and stretched her limbs in bed.

'Shall I ring for the doctor?'

'I—I don't know.'

'But how do you feel?'

'Terrible,' said Maddy's mother.

'I'll ring the doctor, then,' decided Maddy.

'Oh—all right, dear.' Maddy's mother rolled in pain in the bed once again. 'It's Doctor Henderson and his number's in the pad on the table in the hall. You know,' Maddy's mother said to her as she turned to leave the room, 'something terrible's going to happen, something very, very terrible.'

Maddy could not think what her mother meant, and went to lift up the phone. Instead of the familiar dialling tone there was just a noise, like the wind. As though the wind had got stuck in the receiver, somehow. Maddy shook the phone. It was no good. She dialled the operator. No good. Frustrated, she slammed down the phone and shouted back to her mother: 'Phone's not working!' There was a groan from the bedroom. 'Do you want any breakfast?'

'Just—maybe a cup of tea, dear. That'll do me for now. I'm not really hungry.'

Maddy went into the kitchen and filled the kettle. She had a set expression on her face. Somehow, whatever was happening did not seem to be affecting her. Maybe—it must be—Uncle Alistair, Ralph, her dream—oh, the rainbow. Yes, the rainbow and the grandfather clock. The clock in Ralph's hall. Of course. That was where she had seen the rainbow before. It was painted onto the face. A promise it was, a promise and a protection. Ralph's mother had explained it to her. How stupid of her not to have remembered it before. Now she had realised, something seemed to have fallen into place in her mind, though what or why she couldn't have told you if you had asked her. No, not in fifty years.

She took her mother a cup of strong tea. 'I'm going to get Ralph and his uncle,' she said, 'and we'll go round to the doctor's. Will you be all right?'

'I think so.' Maddy's mother nodded weakly and took a mouthful of tea. Maddy half opened the curtains and laid her mother's library book on the edge of her bed. 'Here you are,' she suggested. 'Something to read if you feel up to it.' Maddy popped the front door key into her pocket. 'I hope she'll be all right,' she murmured, 'I do hope she'll be all right!'

Maddy ran all the way through the still-slippery streets and banged hard at Ralph's front door.

'Maddy!' said Ralph.

'Oh, Ralph!' exclaimed Maddy, panting, and not bothering to take off her anorak, 'Mum's ill in bed with something—and—and the phones aren't working.'

'Ours neither,' sympathised Ralph.

'I think she needs to see a doctor,' urged Maddy. She was growing frantic. She was clenching her fists so hard that her knuckles had turned white.

'OK,' said a voice. It was Uncle Alistair, his mouth rimmed white with toothpaste, brush in hand, 'We'll be right there.'

The clouds were beginning to close their fingers over the sky again as they walked along the road. Even the trees appeared to be drooping, burdened by some mysterious weight. Outside, it was just like the day before. Curtains were closed and there were few people about.

Maddy, Ralph and Uncle Alistair walked through the cathedral close and on into town—where... What a change had come about in just two days! Instead of the usual throng of people, chatting and shopping, there was now only a dribble of isolated shoppers looking worried and defensive. Hardly a word was spoken. Some of the smaller shops had closed altogether DUE TO ILLNESS, while the fountain and benches were littered with individuals just sitting and staring into space. They were open-mouthed. Not moving. It was as if they had been emptied somehow—of everything. As though their memories had gone. The scene was chill, frightening, macabre.

Maddy and Ralph clutched nervously at Uncle Alistair as though he were some kind of charm or protection against all that was happening, and they whispered: 'What is it? What is it? What's happening?'

'I don't quite know—yet,' answered Uncle Alistair, and he gave both of them a squeeze. 'But try not to worry too much. Remember, after the storm—there's a rainbow.'

'Ah, a rainbow!' echoed Maddy. Yes, the rainbow. There was that rainbow again.

Dr Henderson's surgery was down a side street next to an architect's office. The door was open and there was a light on inside.

'At least there is life here,' commented Uncle Alistair. As they stepped over the threshold they met the fresh, sharp smell of disinfectant, and—behind a window—a portly woman in a white coat sitting on a swivel chair. Her glasses hung on a chain round her neck and she was scribbling something on a pad.

'Good morning,' said Uncle Alistair.

'Is it?' replied the receptionist, with a sharp glance at Uncle Alistair. 'The phones are down and there's a queue of people a mile long waiting to see the doctor.'

'Ah, we—er—came about this young lady's mother. She's not well.'

'Nobody's well!' shrugged the receptionist. 'What are the symptoms?'

Uncle Alistair pushed Maddy up to the window. 'Well, she's—er—tired and has no energy and can't get up. And she's frightened of something.'

'That's it!' the woman cried, slamming her pen down on the table. 'Fear—that's what's at the bottom of this. Fear has got this town in its grip.'

'But it doesn't appear to have you in its grip,' remarked Uncle Alistair, giving the woman an odd look.

'Let's just say that some of us know how to deal with these things.' And she gave Uncle Alistair such an odd look in return that he crimsoned slightly.

At that moment Ralph noticed that she was wearing a rainbow bangle and it made him jump. There it was again.

'Is Dr Henderson not available then?' asked Uncle Alistair, returning to his more normal manner.

'Dr Henderson is in bed—like almost everyone else. However, two doctors have come up from Southampton, though one of them isn't feeling too good now either. I can have an ambulance sent round...'

'How, if the phones are down?' interrupted Uncle Alistair.

'Walkie-talkie,' the woman said. 'And we can send the girl's mother to Southampton for observation. The beds are full to overflowing here. Believe me, that would be THE BEST THING. I have a feeling that Southampton air will effect a quick cure.'

'I'm sure you're right,' agreed Uncle Alistair.

'I'm sure I am,' replied the woman. 'Jot down the name

and address here, and give me half an hour. You realise I'm only doing this for you.'

'I think so,' said Uncle Alistair.

'Goodbye then,' murmured the receptionist. 'I'm sure we'll win through. Hope and persistence, hope and persistence, that's what we need.' She swivelled round and continued her work. Ralph turned once more to stare at the woman's bangle as they left the surgery.

'What a strange woman,' said Maddy. 'Did you know her?'

'No,' mused Uncle Alistair, 'but she did, on the other hand, appear to guess something important about me.'

The ambulance came about half an hour later. Maddy had put some things into a bag for her mother and, as the two men put her onto a stretcher, she pressed Maddy's hand. 'Be good,' she said, and she gave Uncle Alistair a weak smile.

'We all have need of the good now,' he answered. 'Light to drive back the dark.' He smiled back—and his strong smile seemed to warm and comfort Maddy's mother.

Maddy waved from the pavement outside as the ambulance set off. She waved till it had gone right out of sight.

'Your mother's safe now,' said Uncle Alistair. 'Very safe. The moment she arrives in Southampton she will begin to grow well again. Do you understand? It is here, in the air and in the streets that the sickness is.'

Maddy nodded dumbly.

'You ready?' asked Ralph, and Maddy nipped back upstairs to collect clothes and a toothbrush and to lock the door behind her.

'It's better if you are with us anyway,' soothed Uncle Alistair. 'It's safer.'

Maddy tried to smile, but her mind was on other

71

things. Her mother's worn face. Her mother's weak smile. They haunted her as she walked the two streets back to Ralph's house with Ralph and Uncle Alistair. Her intentness dampened the conversation and they proceeded mainly in silence. It was at that moment, as Ralph listened, that he realised even the birds had stopped singing. And just at that moment Uncle Alistair held out his arm as a barrier, forcing them to stop.

'Oh, no!' Maddy gasped. Ralph blanched and swallowed hard. A great fist seemed to have taken hold of his stomach and was squeezing it tight.

'Not us too!' he cried. For there, daubed on the pavement in front of Ralph's house, were some characters of strange design splashed in yellow paint.

7

Ralph and Maddy swallowed hard and took a step into the road, wondering what they should do.

'Hold on a minute!' ordered Uncle Alistair sternly.

The row of yellow symbols on the pavement leered up at them, challenging them to cross.

'Now, listen,' he explained. 'I've discovered a lot in the last twenty-four hours. The papers the man gave me at Marchbury House were very useful. They have explained and revealed a great deal. But there are things that are deeper and more powerful than magic. Watch this!' Uncle Alistair spread his arms out in front of him and lifted his head till his chin seemed to point straight at the letters.

There was a deathly pause, as if scales were balanced, not knowing which way to tip—then a rush, a gust of chilling wind. The row of yellow symbols shivered momentarily, as if they were afraid. Then, to Ralph's and Maddy's astonishment, they scattered and ran like a pack of frightened rabbits. Under the hedge, into the gutter, right to the foot of the lamp post, pieces of the letters detached themselves and, changing once more into paint, dissolved and dribbled, harmless, their power broken.

'Now we can go inside,' said Uncle Alistair more easily, 'and I *don't* think this will happen again.'

Maddy and Ralph followed him dumbly, banging their cold feet on the doormat to force some warmth into them. Uncle Alistair fumbled with the key. Once inside, it soon became clear to them that some things were working, but others were not. The radio was working, for one thing, but the phones were not. The newspaper had been delivered, though, but it was one of those free ones that gets pushed through everyone's door. Maddy unrolled the paper. Underneath FREWIN DAM NEARS COMPLETION, she spotted LOCAL WOMAN SIGHTS DRAGON: 'Mrs L. Keensby of 51, Warren Avenue, yesterday claimed that a real, live dragon flew in and sat on her washing-line. "It was terrifying," claimed Mrs Keensby, 34, and mother of two. "I was nearly scared out of my wits..."'

'Look,' said Maddy, putting the newspaper into Uncle Alistair's hand, 'do you think that this can be true?'

'Maybe,' frowned Uncle Alistair. 'On the other hand, it could just be the result of the way everybody's feeling. Who knows?' He shrugged. And then... Maddy remembered her dream. There had been a dragon in that—one of the ominous beasts unleashed by the black cat. She shivered.

'Now, you two,' said Uncle Alistair, 'I have some more translating to do before lunch, so you'll have to amuse yourselves.' He disappeared to his room and they heard the bang as a bedroom door closed behind him.

'He's been on it all night!' exclaimed Ralph, amazed that anyone could work so hard.

'What?' said Maddy, kneeling down on the carpet and switching on the television. Ralph opened a drawer and rummaged around for a pack of cards. 'Translating—the bits of that book. The sheets he got from the man at Marchbury House.'

'Oh, the man he hypnotised—or whatever it was.'

They sat down to play cards, with the TV as background noise. Whist and rummy, for an hour. Ralph won the whist and Maddy won the rummy. She was just about to take the last trick with the Queen of Spades when Uncle Alistair poked his head round the door.

'Busy?' he asked.

'Mine,' said Maddy, taking the last trick and winning the game.

'Now,' began Uncle Alistair, coming in with a sheaf of papers in his hand, and round, gold-rimmed glasses perched on the end of his nose, 'I will tell you what I have discovered. It is all very interesting.' He sat down, tall and magisterial on the sofa.

'First,' announced Uncle Alistair, 'I want to get rid of any unwanted visitors.'

'Visitors?' queried Ralph, looking round.

'Don't be fooled into thinking that all the visitors we have are ones we can see. Besides . . .'

'Oh, look!' cried Maddy, pointing at the window. For there, balanced on the ledge outside, was Mrs Morgan's black cat. It rubbed its side against the pane and hissed, its glittery green eyes scanning the scene in front of it.

'Precisely,' said Uncle Alistair, taking his point as proved. 'You see . . .' Chewing his lip, he waited for a moment, facing the window, until silence fell on the room. Then—he clapped his hands, and in a very loud voice shouted out: 'Go! Go, and don't come back!' The windows of the living-room shook, as at a thunder-clap, and the cat gave a yowl—as if someone had struck it with a red-hot poker—and jumped away.

'That'll teach her,' chuckled Uncle Alistair. 'But, it will also *show* her that we know something, and the problem is that we still do not know what we know. If the truth be known, none of us really knows what is going on. Or why. But listen, here's a clue.'

Maddy glanced nervously at the window.

'Don't worry,' reassured Uncle Alistair, 'the cat won't come back. It can't. We're protected now. Magic. No, more than magic. Something Mrs Morgan and her kind hate so much, they would do anything to destroy it—only it is too much for them.'

Downstairs in the hall Ralph thought that the grand-father clock had somehow increased its tick. Measuring time. Keeping time. Measuring. Keeping. Measuring. Guarding. Keeping.

'Apart from a bundle of spells—the usual how-to-cure-warts, how-to-make-a-dry-cow-give-milk, and how to have a baby if you want one—there are one or two notable spells of power. Unusual spells. Spells such as—how to raise the leviathan, how to call down fire, how to strike down armies, that kind of thing. Now,' Ralph and Maddy adjusted themselves into more comfortable positions and went on listening, 'more, well not more, but in a different way, interesting, is the *history* included in the book. The monk who copied down the spells was one person, but, later on—much later on, someone else has seen fit to write a story on the last pages in, if I am not mistaken, seventeenth century hand-writing. It is most fascinating. Listen. Are you sitting comfortably? Then let he (or she) who has an ear, hear—'

'Just a minute!' interrupted Maddy.

'What?' asked Uncle Alistair a little irritably. Ralph knew that his uncle did not like anyone breaking into his important moments, especially when he was about to tell a story.

'What's a leviathan?'

'It's a big snake, like a water-monster. People used to believe that it went round the middle of the world like a belt and that its mouth gripped hold of its tail—now, listen!'

Maddy gulped and shifted uncomfortably—for she had dreamed about that too.

'And in the year of Our Lord sixteen hundred and forty-seven, it came to pass that there was a fearsome blight of witchcraft in the land. So great was the iniquity of these women that many godly folk were stricken with fever and died.

'Now there was no more zealous soldier for the Lord than Sir Oliver Marchbury. He raised up the standard of God and fought the devil and all his instruments of darkness and yea, for three years, under his hand, many were brought to trial and accused and condemned to death. At first the lesser women were hung by the neck till they were dead, but those found to have been consorting with the devil himself were burned for the sake of their souls. And it came to pass that Marchbury at last accused even his own sister Margaret of inciting evil spells and wickednesses.

'Soon after, it happened that he fell sick and was near unto death. But an angel of the Lord came and watched over him, and thus it was that Marchbury did not die, but recovered the strength of his limbs and, with it, the stoutness of his heart. He called for an examination to be held at the courthouse and many there were who came to hear it.

'Margaret spoke not one word throughout her trial, not one word, but kept her head bowed to the earth. The evidence arraigned against her was terrible indeed. For Marchbury claimed that his sister had ridden with the devil through the air on a broom, and that she had taken the form of a cat. He called forth several witnesses who testified to this, including Margaret's own maid of several years. The court were full astonished and after but a short adjournment returned the sound verdict of guilty. Margaret and two others were taken to the marketplace to be burned. Marchbury held aloft the death warrant, but his sister refused to look at it, so deep was her guilt.

'After some prayers in which the minister of the gospel sought mercy from Almighty God and thanked him for delivering up these three witches to judgement, a torch kindled the bonfires and the three women were consigned to the flames. Marchbury gazed on his doomed sister, and

77

uttered only one word—"Morgana"—which word sore amazed the judge standing beside him. For was not his sister's name Margaret? But she turned to him and cried out in a loud voice that all might hear: "I stand accused and punished in this place. And by fire or water I will bring down destruction upon you. If not in this generation, then in the generations to come!"

'At these words Marchbury was seized with a mighty trembling and could barely restrain himself. The following morning he was moved to inspect the place of burning to ensure to himself that the three women were truly dead. But the report of one man alarmed him, for this man, one John Matthews, did swear under oath that he had espied three crows flying away from the market-place while the flames were at their height.

'At this Marchbury was grievously affrighted and soon after, in the space of three days from the burning, he took once more to his bed. The fever settled for a second time on his limbs and he died, full of worms and other creeping things. Only then, at his death, was the great plague of witchcraft in the land at last abated.'

Uncle Alistair halted and cleared his throat. His glasses had slid almost to the end of his nose, and the hush in the room had sunk right down inside Maddy and Ralph, to their very toes.

'So, did she really die?' asked Ralph. 'And was she really a witch?'

'I think she had power,' returned Uncle Alistair slowly and thoughtfully, 'and the power consumed her. Badness is like a slide, you see. Once you've started it's hard to stop. Her brother was not wholly good, though. Many of those women he called witches were no doubt innocent and had never harmed anyone more than giving them some herb broth when they were ill.'

'I don't understand,' said Maddy, shaking her head and

looking at the carpet. 'I don't understand at all.' And she thought of her mother again, saying that they had all been bad, that they had all done something wrong. And how she had not known what her mother had meant. How could they all be bad? She was heavy, dizzy all of a sudden. 'How can someone die and come back? It isn't possible.'

'We've seen a lot of things happen in the last couple of days that seem impossible to us. We don't know how—but how is not as important as *why*.'

'Morgana,' repeated Ralph. 'Mrs Morgan. It all fits.'

'No.' Uncle Alistair shook his head. 'Unfortunately it does not all fit. We only have scraps, pieces of a puzzle that we must join together and soon, for time is running out.'

'Who was Morgana?' asked Maddy.

'Ah, that's easy enough. Morgan Le Fay was King Arthur's half-sister and a very powerful witch.'

'And Vivien?' added Ralph. 'Didn't it say "Vivien Morgan" on the package we saw at her house?'

'Right enough. Vivien was a young witch who tricked Merlin, the wizard at King Arthur's court, into going into a cave. Then she sealed up the cave with him inside and left him there—for ever—after she had learned the secrets of his power.'

'How awful!' said Maddy. 'Is he still there?'

'Perhaps,' mused Uncle Alistair, 'but I wouldn't lose any sleep over it. These are just names—though names are often clues.'

'Why do you say time is running out?' asked Ralph sharply, his uncle's words just sinking in. Uncle Alistair cleared his throat again and sat back in the sofa. 'The really powerful spells take place on the night of the full moon.'

'Yes?' said Maddy, blinking and leaning forward.

'Well, it just so happens that the full moon is tomorrow night. Whatever it is we have to stop must be stopped before midnight tomorrow. Or it really will be too late!'

8

The nastiness of the story Uncle Alistair had read out loud hung in all their minds. Lunch passed in an uncomfortable silence, with only the sweet aroma of baked beans and the blare of the radio filling the space. The kitchen curtains flapped half-heartedly at the partly open window, like the wings of a tired bird. Outside, there was only stillness. No washing blowing. No cars. No children playing. No old people chatting. Nothing. It was as if someone had come along with a mighty broom and swept all the streets clean. Maddy was worried about her mother. The phones still weren't working, so it was impossible to contact the hospital and ...

'... now for some local news. Owing to a freak storm earlier today, the A33, about 20 miles north of South-ampton, has been blocked by a landslide. Workmen have been seriously hindered in their efforts to begin clearing the earth and rubble, as a tanker collided with two cars and overturned. No one was hurt, but the police advise those travelling to Southampton today to take an alternative route. A gas leak near Andover has ...'

Uncle Alistair clicked the radio off. 'I don't think we want any more of that,' he said. 'We know what's happening.'

'My mother!' started Maddy with widened eyes.

'... is quite safe,' soothed Uncle Alistair. 'Her ambu-lance must definitely have got through by now.'

'You mean we can't get out?' said Ralph.

'No one wants to get out anyway,' muttered Maddy, going to the window and looking over the garden to the quiet houses and flats beyond.

'Yes, we're being fenced in, slowly but surely. It must be a preparation.'

'I don't see,' ground Maddy through her teeth, 'how we can do anything at all if we don't know anything. I mean, we don't know *anything*.'

'Ah,' said Uncle Alistair, pointing a finger at Maddy and fixing her with a stare, 'we do know that *something's* happening, and that puts us one step ahead of everybody else.'

Maddy sighed, shoulders sagging, and Ralph put all his concentration into trying to balance as many baked beans on the end of his knife as he could.

'Tea?' asked Uncle Alistair encouragingly, but neither Maddy nor Ralph felt much like it.

'If the television goes,' muttered Ralph darkly, 'that really will be the end.'

Uncle Alistair gave Ralph one of those looks that grown-ups give children when they want to complain about the younger generation. Not that Uncle Alistair appeared to belong to any particular generation himself.

After lunch Uncle Alistair stretched out his long legs in the living-room and began to read the newspaper. The big news was the Frewin Dam. It had been taking years to build and would provide water for the towns and villages for miles around. The authorities were trying to think of someone really important who could come and open it: now they were all fighting about who this should be. It was the usual thing. Ralph and Maddy had been taken to see the site on a class trip, and it had all been explained by an earnest young man with a pointer, some diagrams, and a video.

It was a shame about flooding the village though, even

if nobody did live there nowadays. The ruins were a popular picnic spot, and the birdwatchers who came there in the summer had written a great many letters to complain. But it was too late now. Frewin Dam was a fact, and three months from now it would be open and working. Uncle Alistair yawned. Dams were not his thing. Dragons now, they were something else, and his keen eyes scanned the account of Mrs Keensby and her sighting.

'That's funny!' Maddy suddenly remarked.

'What?' asked Ralph, rising to his feet. He had been trying to build a house out of cards, a favourite after-lunch occupation.

'It's Mrs Morgan,' continued Maddy. 'Down there.' She indicated with her head.

'Is it indeed!' exclaimed Uncle Alistair, showing some interest. He was suddenly livelier than he had been all day. 'Let me see.' He stood sideways on to the window, behind the curtains, and watched as a figure hurried by below them. It was Mrs Morgan all right. And her tread showed determination. She was wearing a buttoned-up coat with a fur collar, a kind of granny coat—and flat, lace-up black shoes. Her umbrella was folded like a crow under one arm and a carpet bag swung from the other. And she was wearing a hat, a fur one, pulled right down over her forehead.

'I wonder where she's going?' said Ralph.

'To make mischief most likely,' answered Uncle Alistair, 'but it would be too dangerous to follow her now. Especially as the streets are so empty. She is clever, whatever else she may be. Still...' He picked up his shoes which were lying at the foot of the sofa and rubbed the dust off them with his fingers, 'if she's not in, then she's...'

'Out,' finished Ralph. 'So?'

'So now is the perfect time to pay her a little visit. After all, nobody will see us because, as is perfectly apparent, nobody is there. Nobody is anywhere.'

'But ... isn't that ... burglary?' protested Maddy, astonished. 'I mean, we just can't ... climb in through her window.'

'That is precisely what I intend to do.' Uncle Alistair bent over and laced up both his shoes.

'But she might come back!' persisted Maddy with some frustration.

'In that case we must have a plan.'

'Which is?' demanded Ralph, eyeing his uncle and crossing his arms resolutely in front of his chest.

'Which is ... Maddy keeps watch at the side of the house while you and I go inside. The moment Mrs Morgan appears—and you can see quite a long way down the road—Maddy gives us a warning signal.'

'What warning signal?'

'You run round the back of the house and knock very loudly on the window.'

'It sounds a bit dangerous to me,' said Maddy.

'Don't get me wrong,' declared Uncle Alistair with some firmness. 'I am not saying that we should use a little evil to do some good: that would never do at all. That isn't how things work. It you do that, evil just leads to more evil and eventually the good withers away as—expedient. Right now we're like policemen on an investigation—we have a right to find out if there is anything in that house that can help us. Now, are you coming or not?' His face was slightly flushed and his eyes were bright. 'There is no time,' he continued, 'for nonsense!'

'I suppose so,' mumbled Maddy, though she still looked uncomfortable.

'We'll come,' agreed Ralph, though it was clear that he did not like the idea either.

'No need for coats!' ordered Uncle Alistair. 'It's only next door, after all.'

Maddy and Ralph put on their outdoor shoes in the hall, mechanically and in silence. Uncle Alistair hovered over them impatiently, drumming his fingers on the piano lid. The clock ticked. The only regular sound in the house. When they were ready, Uncle Alistair opened the front door and they walked quickly round to the back of the house and climbed over the wall. Normally there were hundreds of windows, like eyes, to watch them. But today they knew that all those eyes were shut.

Next door, Mrs Morgan's house had a long, rectangular lawn. It led to a shed at the bottom that leaned against the high wall which hemmed in the whole of the garden. The daffodils were out, drugged and uncaring, waving in the shivery wind that was blowing. It was cold. Colder here, it seemed, than it was in Ralph's garden.

There were three windows at the back of Mrs Morgan's house. One, belonging to a toilet, was frosted, small and open—but too tiny to get in. There was a sort of study room, but the window to that was jammed tight. And then there was the kitchen window. The small window at the top, the one to let the steam and smells out, was open, although the bigger one was shut.

'Just what we need!' breathed Uncle Alistair with satisfaction.

'What do you want us to do?' Ralph asked. Without a coat, he was shaking with cold.

'I want you to climb inside, of course. But first we must make sure that there aren't going to be any surprises.' Uncle Alistair clapped his hands three times, uttered one word—a word of power—that seemed to hang in the air as though it were palpable and real, and then, with a sign, he sent it flying into the house. 'That should do the trick!' he laughed. He squatted down on the concrete path to let Ralph scramble onto his shoulders. Swaying a little, he stood up straight, so that Ralph could reach the high-up window. Ralph put his hand down inside, straining with his fingers to catch hold of the handle of the larger window.

'Higher!' he whispered. 'Higher!'

A drop of sweat appeared on Uncle Alistair's forehead as he strained up on tiptoe. Ralph's hand sank further behind the glass. 'I still can't reach it!' he hissed. 'You'll have to go higher. Just an inch more!'

'An inch?' thought Uncle Alistair. It was like drowning a foot from the shore. With a deep breath, Uncle Alistair tensed himself and gave a heave. Ralph's hand jerked downwards and caught hold of the handle. It squeaked as he turned it.

'Good boy!' applauded Uncle Alistair encouragingly. Lightly, he let Ralph back down onto the path, and reached to ease the window open. It opened outwards. The ledge just inside, over the sink, was full of empty milk bottles and jam jars, cloths and a bottle of washing-up liquid.

'We'll have to be careful,' warned Uncle Alistair. He had got his knees onto the outside sill of the window. Carefully he lifted himself in. He helped Ralph in quickly after him.

'What about the cat?' asked Ralph.

'Don't be silly,' said Uncle Alistair. 'Now.'

'What are we looking for?' whispered Ralph.

'What are we whispering for?' asked his uncle in a normal, everyday voice.

'Because this is somebody else's house!' retorted Ralph.

Uncle Alistair shrugged. He looked quite at home. 'Anything,' he said, 'anything that can help us. That's what we're looking for.'

There was nothing in the kitchen. Only formica work-tops and cupboards, a pile of plates, an ironing-board and an empty laundry basket. Uncle Alistair walked through into the tidy living-room, but there was nothing out of the ordinary in there either. Then he went upstairs to have a nose around.

Maddy was crouching at the side of the house under the eaves, feeling worried sick. Her eyes darted this way and that, first down one side of the road and then down the other. The gap between the high hedge at the front of the house and the wall made it possible to see at a distance, but close up everything was hidden. What if Mrs Morgan came round the corner of Walthamstow Road unexpectedly? They were all sure to be caught then. It is always the same when you feel that you are doing something wrong—you think someone is likely to pop up at the very worst moment.

Ralph heard the creak of the floorboards under his uncle's feet upstairs as he glanced at the litter of papers in Mrs Morgan's study. There wasn't much in there. A table at the window to work on, a chest-of-drawers with some of the drawers half open, and a bureau standing against the wall by the door. Ralph picked up some of the papers and began to examine them. He knew that nothing should look disturbed. As he glanced down, he noticed a map lying half-draped over one end of the table. It was an Ordnance Survey map of the area: one of those detailed ones that divides everything into neat squares. There were crosses marked on it. Ralph moved stealthily to the foot of the stairs.

'Come quick!' he called. 'I think I've found something!'

Quick as a flash, Uncle Alistair left or abandoned his fruitless searching upstairs and hurried down to see what Ralph had discovered.

Ralph took him into the study and lifted one end of the map.

'Interesting,' pronounced Uncle Alistair, and put his finger on a couple of places. 'She's written on it too. Look, landslide here—gas leak there. Mmm, very efficient. But, what's this here? Do you know this place, Ralph? It's close by.'

Ralph bent over the map and peered into the square that Uncle Alistair was pointing to. 'Of course!' he squealed, banging on the side of his head with his fist. 'Of course! How stupid of me! I should have known!'

'Known what?' Uncle Alistair waited impatiently for an explanation.

'Witches' Height! The name of that place is Witches' Height! It's where they all go on Hallowe'en to dance.'

'Indeed?' murmured Uncle Alistair, with a lift of his eyebrows. 'Now, what can she be doing there?'

'Casting spells, of course!' exclaimed Ralph, astonished that his uncle had not twigged. 'That's where they go to do it. Around here, that is. That's the story, anyway.'

'Mmm,' said Uncle Alistair, 'some stories are true—unfortunately. Now, is there anything else?'

Maddy felt as if her eyes would glaze over, she was trying so hard not to blink. She shivered. She should have brought her coat and... wait a minute... There was a speck further down the road... coming this way... with a bag and an umbrella... It was...

'A diary,' noted Uncle Alistair, pulling a slim blue hard-backed book from under the map. 'With the moon in it—naturally. Now, there are dates marked here. And... W.H.—that must be Witches' Height. Let's see,' he flicked through several of the pages, '11 o'clock. 11 o'clock. 11 o'clock. I presume she means at night. And tonight too. 11 o'clock. Fire. I wonder what that means? And tomorrow. 12 o'clock. Water. That doesn't sound too good, either. Fire. Water.'

'It sounds like that story you read to us out of the book of spells.'

'It does indeed,' agreed Uncle Alistair. 'Not very comforting, is it? Fire. Water. And tomorrow is the night of the full moon. Oh, there's nothing written in after that. Well...'

Bang! Bang! Ralph and his uncle both stiffened and went white. They looked at the window. But it was only Maddy telling them to hurry up. She waved urgently.

'We'd better go, Ralph,' Uncle Alistair said. 'Quick!' They hurried back into the kitchen and Uncle Alistair bundled Ralph out of the window. Then he tried to lever himself out and—kicked over a jam jar by the sink. It fell outside. Maddy caught it. They let out a long breath.

'That was close,' murmured Ralph with relief.

By now Mrs Morgan was not so much a speck as a blot, striding down the street, using her umbrella as a kind of cane. She stopped for a moment to sniff the air, and her eyes narrowed.

Balancing on his uncle's shoulders, Ralph reached through the top window again to fasten the catch below—and the three of them edged along Mrs Morgan's garden wall to the point where they could scramble over it. They sat down on the wet grass on their own side, knees scuffed and dusty, breathing heavily.

'Let's wait here a minute,' said Uncle Alistair, 'till she goes inside. If we make a move now she might see us.'

They huddled against the wall and waited till they heard the creaking swing of her iron gate and then the slam of the front door closing.

'Now!' urged Uncle Alistair, and the three of them charged across the lawn. They raced round the side of the house and up to the front door.

Maddy and Ralph flopped into the hall.

'I never want to do that again!' declared Ralph, panting. He marched upstairs.

'I thought she was going to come back any minute!' Maddy was shaking. 'I was frightened!'

'You both did very well,' said Uncle Alistair.

'Did we?' Ralph was half-way up the stairs and poked his head through the wooden bars of the banister. 'Did we *really*?'

'Very well,' repeated Uncle Alistair.

'At least we're safe here,' commented Maddy.

'For the time being anyway,' remarked Uncle Alistair dubiously. They followed him into the living-room.

'But what now?' said Ralph.

'You read the diary,' said Uncle Alistair, chewing a fingernail. 'We found a diary,' he explained to Maddy. 'Witches' Height, 11 o'clock. Fire. Mrs Morgan will be there. We'll just have to make sure that we are, too!'

9

'Have you got a torch?' asked Uncle Alistair. He was standing beside the kitchen table and had changed into an old shirt and thick, cord trousers. It was dark outside now and the curtains were shut.

'Think so,' answered Ralph.

'Well, make sure. We need one. And what about your feet?'

'I've got wellingtons,' said Ralph.

'So have I,' chipped in Maddy, 'but they're back at the flat.'

'Then we'll have to stop off on our way. I don't want you two catching cold, quite apart from anything else.' Exactly what the 'anything else' was, Uncle Alistair did not go on to say.

'Torch, map, thick jackets,' he mumbled to himself, ticking off the list he had scribbled down, 'whistle, notebook and pen, woolly hats and gloves—it will be cold out there.'

'Downstairs in the hall,' waved Ralph. 'All that sort of stuff is there.'

'Then let's see what we can find. Are you ready?'

Both Maddy and Ralph took a very deep breath and nodded. Ready for what, though? For fire? What did that mean?

'It's quiet outside,' said Ralph, lifting up one edge of the curtain, '. . . still. There's nothing moving at all.'

'Is there a light on in Mrs Morgan's house?' asked Ralph's uncle.

'Yes.'

'Good. Then the coast, as they say, is clear, and we must be on our way. We ought to leave some lights on to throw her off the track.'

'But what if she's done the same to us?' asked Maddy.

'I don't think she will have.'

'But won't she have noticed that someone has been in her house?'

'Maybe, but she can't be sure. You see, I had to knock down a very big wall—not a wall of stone, of course, to get inside. And then build it up again after we came out. That was difficult, but I did it. She may have smelt us, or sensed us though . . .'

'Smelt us!' exclaimed Maddy in disgust. She leaned forward on her chair and began spreading a slice of bread with margarine and peanut butter.

'People like Mrs Morgan have good noses,' explained Uncle Alistair. 'They can smell anyone, or anything, a mile off. Sometimes they can smell the future.'

'Hmph!' was all Ralph had to say.

'But you see,' went on Uncle Alistair, 'even if she does suspect that someone has been in her house, she won't know if they found the map or the diary and if they understood them. And she won't know that we know she's planning something big, a finale for tomorrow night.'

'I hope you're right,' frowned Ralph. 'I don't want to end up being captured by a witch!'

'I don't think,' said Uncle Alistair, 'that any of us does.' He counted the items laid out on the kitchen table once more, going over them in his mind—then they all went downstairs to find their jackets.

'What's the time?' asked Maddy.

'Time to go,' said Ralph. It was half-past nine by the grandfather clock. Its careful and steady tick resounded through the house.

The street outside was dark and damp. The pavement and road were shiny under the dusty orange street lamps that cast such a strange glow over everything. The trees were bent and drooping, gathered masses of shadow that seemed ready to take on any form—while the grass was heavy and wet from the day's rain. Lights were on in the houses. Warm lights, welcoming through the curtains, oblong lights of blue and pink and yellow, showing life in the dark. There were people there still. But inside. And who knew what was happening to them? For hardly anyone had been out all day. Ralph glanced up at all the windows. He wondered. One thing he knew—outside it was quiet, eerily quiet.

They went to Queen's Gate Street first, to pick up Maddy's wellingtons and check the flat. Everything was in its place: nothing tampered with. Except that the rooms were unheated and chilly, with no one there all day. Maddy was a little sad: home was so empty without her mother. As soon as she was ready, however, she bounced to her feet with: 'Which way, then?'

'You've got the map in your jacket pocket,' said Uncle Alistair to Ralph. 'Let's have a look,' and they spread it out on the floor.

'Down here,' pointed Ralph.

'No,' Uncle Alistair shook his head. 'I don't want to go by the road. It's too dangerous. For all we know she may have appointed guards and, besides, that's probably the way she'll come. No, I want to get there across country. That's why we've brought the torch and dressed up as though we're on a commando raid.'

Maddy chewed her forefinger and then said brightly, 'I know—down by the river—that is, the other way from Marchbury House, and we can go up Pig's Hill. There's a path. We went down there last summer. We should be able to get up to Witches' Height easily enough from there.'

Uncle Alistair looked at Ralph for confirmation, and Ralph agreed.

'Yes, I've been that way too. But it's not the shortest.'

'We don't want the shortest,' said Uncle Alistair, folding the map with some difficulty (why is it that maps never will fold up properly?). 'We want the safest.'

They opened the door of Maddy's flat and walked down the brightly-lit stairs.

'You'd better lead the way,' suggested Uncle Alistair, 'as you seem to know it.' And once more they were out in the night.

Some nights are comfortable, soothing and safe. They are warm and dry and full of the scents of flowers. They are for being peaceful and still in. For enjoying, for savouring, like some long, pleasing drink that only comes at special times of the year. But not this night. It was wet with puddles after the rain, and had a smell of something not-quite-pleasant in the air. The sky above had no stars, and an almost-full moon struggled out from behind thick clouds. It was as if the night had been rolled in something even darker than usual, or else someone had taken hold of the whole world, like an orange, and was beginning to squeeze it with a great, black fist.

Whatever it was, they all felt uncomfortable, like musical instruments that have been too finely strung, and this made it difficult to make conversation as they walked along. One side of them, the strong, sensible, everyday, daytime one, told them that what they were feeling was nonsense. But another, more hidden side was shivering and seized with panic. And anyway, it was not daytime now, but night. And nothing around them had seemed everyday for quite some time.

They reached the meadow gate and climbed over it. The ground was spongy and soft under their boots as they made their way across the deserted open space to the river's edge. The water swirled by their feet, wide and fast in the gloom. A way off, the winking orange and white lights of street lamps and houses fringed the horizon as they began to walk along the unlit path by the side of the river. On the other side there were houses and then a wood—then a field and a hill and, finally, no houses at all. Beside them was the meadow.

'That's Pig's Hill over there!' hissed Maddy suddenly in the darkness. Her voice cut the silence.

'I see,' said Uncle Alistair slowly, 'and how do we ... ?'

'There's a bridge,' Ralph broke in quickly. He looked around.

'Don't worry,' said Uncle Alistair, 'we're not likely to meet anybody—well, maybe only *one* person, and certainly not here. Now, what time is it?'

Ralph shone the torch on his watch. 'Ten past ten,' he announced.

'Then we must get a move on,' urged Uncle Alistair. 'Come on.'

They walked a few yards more, till they came to a long wooden bridge with a gate at each end. They crossed the river, followed the path on the other side for a little way, climbed a stile, and began to cross the field that led up the back of Pig's Hill. The hill was not very difficult to conquer. Pig's Hill was a local high spot, where picnickers came for the view, and there were a few empty benches on the top. On a good day you could see right across Fitzknowe to Frewin, where the dam was.

'Which way now?' asked Uncle Alistair.

'Along here,' pointed Maddy, 'I think, or ... Everything looks the same in the dark.'

'No, it's down here,' indicated Ralph, facing in another direction. 'I remember now. This way,' and he waved Maddy and his uncle to follow him. The hill dipped down on the far side of them, to a car park. Striking out to the left, they moved down the grassy slope to a belt of trees. Ralph put his hand on his uncle's arm to make him halt.

'Witches' Height is down there,' he said. 'It's round the back of the hill from the town but still high enough for a view.' It was impossible to see much now, but Witches' Height was a sort of lip in the landscape, sheltered by trees on three sides. Stories about it went back a very long way. Stories of green lights on Hallowe'en and the sound of dancing and feasting.

Maddy stood on the other side of Uncle Alistair. 'It *is* down there,' she said, the light wind ruffling her hair. 'I remember now.'

'No talking, then,' urged Uncle Alistair. 'We have to be very careful from now on. I'm trusting you two to show me the way.'

Maddy and Ralph gave each other a quick look of encouragement, and off they tramped with Uncle Alistair following close behind them. They reached the trees easily enough, and brushed against ferns and thorns and dripping undergrowth. Carefully, they pressed on through the shallow wood as quietly as they could until they had almost reached the other side.

Ralph ducked behind a trunk and shone the torch on his watch again. It was ten to eleven. Without a sound, Uncle Alistair came up and seized them both by the arm. He made a vigorous sign to be quiet, and led them to the trunk of a large, sprawling oak. The single-track road came up to the edge of Witches' Height just in front of them and then stopped. It ended in a grassy spot with some picnic tables and rubbish bins, where people came for the view.

There was no one there.

'But it's almost time!' whispered Ralph. Uncle Alistair shook him and gave him such a stern look that he knew not to open his mouth again. Maddy pressed close to Uncle Alistair, partly for reassurance and partly to see better. They waited patiently. There were no animal noises to break the night. Only the rustle of soft under-growth and the drip of already-fallen rain.

Then ... from below ... came the unmistakable noise of an engine revving. Its prolonged growl grew nearer and louder, and suddenly there was the flash of headlights coming up the hill. Bright headlights, like two greedy eyes. The car stopped, its motor dying, and a figure got out. The person lit a cigarette, and, in the momentary glow of the match, it was clear to see what Maddy, Ralph and Uncle Alistair knew well enough already. It was Mrs Morgan. She reached inside the car and took out a small cloth bag, tied at the top. There was something heavy in it. You could tell. And there was something different about her.

Normally she was—well, middle-aged, heavy and small. But tonight she was changed. Younger, wearing crimson high-heeled shoes and an elegant suit. Her hair was cropped short and she was wearing lipstick. She looked out over the calm countryside for a moment, at the scattered ribbons of light beneath, then crushed the cigarette under the sole of her shoe.

Maddy, Ralph and Uncle Alistair waited breathlessly to see what would happen next, pressing a little further round the trunk of the tree. Mrs Morgan went back to her car and took out a shopping-bag. She plumped it down on the middle picnic table and laid the cloth bag beside it. Finally, out of the shopping-bag she took a big, old book. The book. She opened it at a page she had already marked with a piece of card. 'Hmph,' she laughed, a laugh that was more of a grunt, and untied the cloth bag.

Inside it was a stone. Only a stone. The size of an egg. Mrs Morgan consulted her watch, pushing up the sleeve of her jacket. When she was satisfied, she stood at the table behind the book and the stone. Murmuring quietly, she lifted her arms, stretching them out to the night like a priestess, encompassing the whole of the countryside in their width. On she murmured and on, until she appeared to be lost in a kind of trance that had settled on her.

Maddy could feel Ralph's uncle begin to tremble at her side; Ralph felt an uncomfortable tightness in his throat. Louder Mrs Morgan murmured and louder, until the swell of her words reached a climax and dropped away, and she lowered her hands to her sides once again.

All at once, and sudden, there was a break in the cloud, and the bone moon glowered down, grudging its light. A shaft of moonlight, sharp as a knife, fell on the picnic area and bathed Mrs Morgan in its silvery-blueness. With the gleam of a smile she cupped her hands in front of her, letting the light spill off them, and crossed her arms. She rubbed her shoulders, as though she were feeling something tangible and pleasant—and then, with a swift turn of her head, she uttered three loud words that hung, like hovering birds, in the night.

'Go!' cried Mrs Morgan. 'Go!' and the words went, who-knew-where, to do her bidding. Out they went into the night, out, out into the great expanse, and were lost. Vanished in the cloud and the earth and the darkness.

There was silence. A waiting. An intake of breath. And then Maddy tugged at Uncle Alistair's elbow, signalling him to look up. He did so, cautious and puzzled. Ralph's eyes too were drawn to the sky, and he forgot his cramped, uncomfortable position.

For there were lights, like gossamer, like flakes of tinsel, like tiny stars, like leaves, filling the sky and tumbling down, like snowflakes, to the earth. There were hundreds of them, thousands of them, a shower of bright sparks, each it seemed with a life of its own. Down they came and down, and where they touched the earth something sprang up, something sprang to life. Something took form and lived. There was a roar and a bellow, a call and a chirp, a hiss and a growl and a grunt.

Each time a sliver of light touched the ground an animal burst forth, and another noise was added to the yowling and yapping, snapping and snarling that had brutally startled the night. The forms grew and took shape. Legs and heads, fur and teeth, eyes and nails. Large and small, long and squat, tall and minuscule. Each to its appointed shape.

A panther's yellow eyes gleamed in the dark, a wild boar snorted, a dog barked. A magnificent cobra with legs as well as a tail slithered into view, a donkey with two heads and a forked tongue brayed raspingly, and a leopard with a flame flickering out of its mouth bounded into a tree.

There were creatures with flippers, eyes on stalks and long, spiky whiskers.

There was a coil of serpents, two lions and other, terrifying creatures, misshapen and terrible.

The stuff of nightmare.

And they were the creatures in the book... the book that had been in the museum. Ranks of them, rows of them. Hundreds, all crowded together, or so it seemed to Maddy and Ralph. Last of all, from its pages sprang a little silver dragon with saucer eyes. It flapped its bat wings and took its place between a strange cat-like creature with a woman's face and another that had the head of an eagle, the body of a lion and the tail of a snake. Slithering there was, and roaring. Yapping and slavering. Hooves pawed the ground. There was a frightening chorus of growls, bleats, trumpets, hisses and snarls. All of them were there for one thing. Waiting. For one thing. They stood, half-circling Mrs Morgan, who appeared to have grown taller, willowy and majestic. Now she was truly queen of the night. The dark green fire of her eyes burned, holding all of the animals in its power. She was ruler here. At last.

'Silence!' she ordered, and the animals restrained their cries to the occasional snarl or whimper. They pawed the ground, stamping their feet, writhing and hissing. 'The night of nights—the night for which we have waited so long—is at last at hand. This is why I have summoned you here tonight. For the task! For the goal! For the untying!'

Mrs Morgan's voice vibrated like some great organ and her words fell in quivering waves over the heads of her listeners. 'Tonight,' she continued, 'we must call something near to waking. Something that has been asleep for a very long time. We must call up—the leviathan!'

Uncle Alistair was straining, leaning to catch every word. Down he went into himself, opening to the power he belonged to, power deeper and stronger than even Mrs Morgan could imagine, power that went back to the very foundation of the world. That power was the only thing that could protect them now. That power and protection—the rainbow. Uncle Alistair strained, but oh, he felt his strength ebbing.

'Behold!' cried Mrs Morgan, her eyes flashing and her hands outstretched. 'Behold and tremble! For centuries I have slept and waited—waited for this moment. And now I have called you all here to witness the birth—the terrible birth of the end!' Once more she turned, away from the animals, showing her back to them, facing the edge of the Height. She gazed into the sky, letting the moon fill her eyes, her hair, her face—and her slender arms reached up ... The moon seemed to draw her somehow, and then it was as though the light of the moon was tingling and running through her body, like a current of electricity.

'Behold!' she cried again. 'Behold!' And she bent down and picked up the stone from the weather-worn slatted picnic table. In the moonlight, Ralph and Maddy and Uncle Alistair saw her pass her hand over the stone as she muttered more words. She leaned over it, as though embracing it, and then, treating it as some precious thing, she placed the stone back on the table.

'Now!' she cried to the empty darkness. 'Come now! Visit us and take shape! Now! Here! Now!' And, with an almighty gesture, she took one step back, fixing her eyes in concentration on the stone.

The animals shuffled and stamped in their ranks, breathing and panting, and more yapping, growling and whimpering broke out ... only to lapse into silence at Mrs Morgan's restraining hand.

For the moon was changing colour. Something was passing over its cracked and scarred face. A blush, perhaps. Shame at what was happening? Who knew? Who did?

Mrs Morgan.

In the space of just a few moments the moon had crimsoned to a deep red, a dripping, ghastly blood-red ... and then, slowly, the colour faded and the moon turned silver again.

'Ah!'

Mrs Morgan moved her body and shifted her gaze to the black sky above.

'Ah!'

And the animals shivered, unsure and in awe of what was happening in front of them. For, out of the moon, wound a trail of stars, a column, twisting and snaking towards them through the night sky. It was as though the moon were growing a horn. Longer and longer grew the snake-like apparition, nearer and nearer to the earth.

Ralph and Maddy gazed, hypnotized by the sight. They were too terrified to speak or to move, but watched with open mouths as the trail of stars wound closer and closer to the earth.

Uncle Alistair's face was grim in the ghostly, unearthly light. He looked set, as though he were carved in marble, and he did not flinch.

Down came the winding snake of stars, down and down, until the very end tip touched the stone on the picnic table. At once there was a blaze of light ... and the table burst into flames. Ralph, Maddy and Uncle Alistair shut their eyes at the brightness of it, while the animals shifted uneasily and howled and whinnied.

The light was intense, cold and pure, like the heart of a star, engulfing both the table and the stone. Mrs Morgan was transfixed, still as a statue, and in a strange kind of ecstasy. Brighter the light grew, and brighter, till it hurt Ralph, Maddy and Uncle Alistair, even through their eyelids, and they bent down to cover their faces with their hands.

'Aaeeee!' Mrs Morgan let out a scream ... a yell ... a yelp of triumph, and all at once the light began to dim, fading and flickering and shrinking. It grew yellow and orange and then at last dwindled away to nothing. Finally, the only flames left were those licking the embers and ashes of the picnic table which had been completely destroyed.

Unflinching, Mrs Morgan rolled up the sleeve of her left hand and searched about in the nest of yellow flames. When she had found what she was looking for, her hand closed about something hard and certain. She pulled it out and held it close to her chest. Whatever it was, it did not seem to burn her, but rather seemed to be giving her intense pleasure—from the smile on her face, her concentration, her closed eyes ... Then, as she held the object out in front of her, her eyes opened in triumph and her mouth showed mocking delight. She was almost smug. She held the thing up to the moonlight and then swung round to display it to the animals.

It was the stone.

The stone, yes, but changed. It had become white and glittering—a diamond with a light of its own. The moon played strangely on it, stroking it, worrying it—regretfully, it seemed. And its shape had changed. If the shape of the stone had suggested it, the shining diamond confirmed it: the stone had become an egg.

'The egg of leviathan!' announced Mrs Morgan. 'Near now, tomorrow he will be brought to birth, when the

101

moon, his mother, is full. Then will we see such things! Then will we see such marvellous things! What do you say?'

And to her challenge came such a hooting and roaring and neighing and yowling and stamping that Maddy and Ralph thought the whole hill would shake.

'But now you are the forerunners!' declared Mrs Morgan. 'Yours is the time of announcement! Go and do your work!'

And in an instant they were gone. Instead of galloping, running and slithering through the trees and down the hill, the animals turned round and vanished, their heads into their tails, almost as if—after all—they had only been illusions, or bubbles of imagining. Mrs Morgan herself seemed to have diminished, shrunk back to normal size as she took hold of the egg-shaped flashing rock, eerie still in the moonlight. She lifted it and popped it back in the tie-up bag. With a violent scrape of a match, she lit another cigarette, then climbed back into her car, switched on the headlights, coaxed the engine into a metallic roar, reversed, turned and drove away. Only the two red spots of her tail-lights were left to be seen, vanishing into the darkness.

Uncle Alistair pulled Maddy and Ralph to their feet. Ralph's legs hurt and Maddy was stiff all over. All three were wet and cold and aching.

'Is it—is it safe?' asked Maddy uncertainly.

'Yes, it is,' replied Uncle Alistair softly. 'It is—now. Just a few minutes ago it was one of the most dangerous places that anyone has ever been in,' and he gave them a weak smile. He was breathing quickly and looked exhausted.

'What's the matter?' asked Ralph with some concern.

'Nothing, really.' Uncle Alistair held his side for a moment. 'The light—the brightness—we needed a shield against it. It was all I could do to hold ... I asked ... It was—so strong.'

Maddy looked for a stick and walked forward to poke what was left of the picnic table. The mass of glowing red embers keeled over and, with a crackle, a handful of sparks flew up above their heads. 'It's only a fire now,' she said.

'Yes,' affirmed Uncle Alistair, holding out his stiff, frozen hands to the little warmth there was left in the low flames. 'That's all it is now. What's the time?'

It was a quarter to twelve.

'It's going to take us ages to get back,' Maddy said.

'Well, we can't help it,' said Uncle Alistair. 'We needed to be here. One late night won't harm us too much, though we need to be ready and armed for tomorrow. Otherwise, we're all going to go out—right out—just like this fire.' He took Maddy's stick and stirred up a few more sparks from the blackened, charred wood. Then, throwing it away, he led Maddy and Ralph back through the trees and over the fields in the direction of home.

10

Then ... Uncle Alistair rolled over in bed and a low moan sounded from his lips.

Then ... He wrestled with the blankets and shrunk down from the pillow, covering his head up to his ears.

Then ... Uncle Alistair was standing. Standing, looking down. He did not appear to be standing *on* anything, but he was standing. Standing, looking down. At his feet was a shiny pool of salt tears. His tears, shining like a splash of mirror. At his feet. And Uncle Alistair could see his own reflection staring back up at him.

Then the pool grew dark, as if it were no longer a pool, but a hole cut out of the ice—the kind that eskimos fish through. And the pool was underneath, but it was not a pool—it was an ocean, a bottomless ocean. Uncountable fathoms deep. And at the bottom of that ocean, in the dark and the shadows where no sunlight had ever reached, something had awoken.

Whoom! It moved through the water. Uncle Alistair saw its body, thick like the trunk of a tree, going on and on.

Whoom! It travelled, miles long and coiling.

Whoom! Like an arrow. It had awoken from its slumber.

Whoom! Waves of shock vibrated from its body, scaring shoals of smaller fishes and scattering them, flattening the fabulous forests of coral that no one's eyes had ever seen.

Whoom! Stirring up the sand from the bottom of an ocean where no one had ever gone.

Whoom! Two eyes opened and glowed, like pale lanterns, ghostly in the darkness. A fearsome head snaked this way and that, seeking its prey. Smelling for blood. Scenting out the person for whom it had awoken.

Whoom! The creature's green, armour-plated body rose and swam upwards through the water. Nearer the surface it came. Nearer and nearer . . . till it met the faint, lowest rays of the sun where the water cleared. Nearer and nearer, and faster.

Whoom! Whoom!

It shot out of the hole that was the pool of Uncle Alistair's tears and began winding itself about him.

Uncle Alistair staggered and struggled, falling down on to one knee. His breath was constricted. He could not move. The harder he struggled, the more and more tightly the monster squeezed him in its grip. Coil upon coil oozed out of the pool, winding itself round and round him. He felt his face crimson and turn blue. His head swam. He knew he was done for. He could hardly breathe.

In the grip of the monstrous, slimy coils, he bent round and saw for himself the head of the creature. It was grotesque, with a long, protruding jaw and a fringe of fins. It snapped and growled, sending shivers through Uncle Alistair's doomed body. Its eyes were red, smouldering coals of hate, and, as it gazed at Uncle Alistair, he could see that the monster's head was actually the mockery of a human face. His own face. He turned his head away and tried to scream.

He tried to scream and . . . he woke up. It was still gloomy in his bedroom as, with a gasp, he looked at the luminous, pale green face of the alarm clock. Half-past three. Only half-past three. He was cold and shivering. Pulling the blankets up to his shoulder, he lay on his side near the wall and tried to go back to sleep.

'Breakfast is . . .'

'No milk,' replied Ralph ruefully, taking an empty bottle out of the fridge and holding it upside down. One drop fell to the floor.

'Then you'd better go for more,' decided Uncle Alistair. 'I'll give you some money. I suppose it didn't come again this morning.'

'No,' called Maddy from where she was slicing the bread. 'I checked.'

'Ah, well, can you run down to the shop, Ralph, and see if it's open? Be careful, mind.'

'Sure,' said Ralph, gripping the fifty pence piece tightly in his palm and running downstairs.

It was raining again. The sky was blue-grey, as though someone had coloured it in, and all the roofs of the houses were glistening. The lawns sopped like sad sponges, and everything dripped grey—the colour of a TV set whose brightness had been turned down. The front door slammed downstairs.

' . . . a derailment south of Basingstoke this morning has caused severe delays. Passengers are being re-routed from Reading, but the overturned goods train and its load of coal will take many hours to clear. This is the third accident in as many days near . . . crackle . . . crackle . . . crackle . . . and it means that the town is virtually cut off. Telephone services have not been restored, although no fault has been found with the system, and bus services to and from the town have been virtually brought to a standstill. More news when we have it—and now, some music . . .'

It was so wet and grey outside. The kind of day you never would go out in unless you really had to. Maddy was sunk into herself as she cut the bread and put the slices on a china plate. Last night was in all her thoughts, and

106

there were so many questions, questions to which, unfortunately, no one seemed to have any answers.

'Ralph's taking his time,' noticed Uncle Alistair, who was finishing the washing-up from the night before. He stacked the sudsy dishes. 'Do you think he'll be all right?'

'Well, there's no one around,' said Maddy, half-breaking off from her thought for a moment. 'I'll go and see if I can spot him.'

But Maddy was wrong. There was someone around.

'Can you come here?' she shouted through from the living-room. Uncle Alistair wiped his hands on a towel and went to see what the matter was. Maddy was standing by the living-room window with a quizzical look on her face. 'I thought there wasn't anybody,' she said, 'but look, it's Mr Davidson from the History Society. He comes to our school sometimes.'

Uncle Alistair lifted the fine net curtain to see more clearly, and gazed down into the street below. Mr Davidson was walking—loping would be a better word—along the street, and ringing an old handbell. He seemed to have dressed in a hurry, without shaving. His clothes were dishevelled and half undone. As he moved along, every so often he would let out a cry, like an animal of some kind, like a dog. He yowled. Maddy withdrew from the window in confusion, but could not take her eyes away. Now the man was shouting something.

'Open the window!' whispered Maddy. 'I want to hear!'

Uncle Alistair undid the catch of the window and pushed it up with a scrape and a squeak. Rain spattered on to the window-sill inside and the sound of the bell reached into the living-room. 'Unclean!' he was shouting. 'Unclean! We are all doomed! Do-oomed!' And then he yowled again, long and hard, like a dog.

'What—what's the matter with him?' pleaded Maddy, facing Uncle Alistair in frantic astonishment. 'I don't understand—I don't—I . . .'

'Of course!' said Uncle Alistair. 'That's what she meant. Why, Maddy, don't you see ...'

Some people came running out of the houses to greet the man. Three or four of them, grunting and bleating. They stood round him and chatted for a moment, for all the world as normal people do. And then they turned round with a cry and began smashing up one of the cars parked along the road. Its windscreen splintered into a spider's web, collapsing over the inside seats and spilling into the road.

'Maddy!' Uncle Alistair took hold of both her shoulders and turned her towards him. 'It's the animals—don't you see! Mrs Morgan's animals have got in under the skins of the people. All of us have dark, primitive sides, though often we pretend that we haven't, but they are all mixed up with other things. If you let that side come free, if you let it become master, then, terrible things begin to happen ...'

'But the police!' protested Maddy. 'What about them? Surely they can stop it?'

'The chief constable was taken away—don't you remember—and the bishop and the mayor. In fact, every bit of law and order and leadership in the whole town has been struck down in one way or another. They're either in Southampton or in hospital here: and by now the rest of the police probably aren't any better than these folk outside.'

Maddy pressed her hands down hard on the window-sill. The ragged crowd had grown to five or six people. They sniffed the air and staggered off down the street leaving it empty and rainy once again. Only the litter of glass from the windscreen of the car told the tale of what Maddy and Ralph's uncle had just witnessed.

'Oh, goodness! Ralph!' said Uncle Alistair. 'He's not back yet! I must go and look for him! Stay here, and don't let anybody in!' He rushed downstairs to grab his coat and

Maddy saw him, hunched slightly against the rain, disappear down the street to the grocer's. She went back into the kitchen. Breakfast seemed a very dismal affair now. But she dipped a tea-bag in a mug before returned to the living-room window, to sit and wait.

One car had been overturned in the next street. Perhaps Mr Davidson had called here too. But so far there was nobody to be seen. The streets of houses held their impenetrable, eerie silence, closed and shielded from the road, closed from prying eyes and from visitors.

Uncle Alistair reached the grocer's. He was splashed with rain, his hair sticking close to his head, and drops dribbling down his face. It was shut. ILLNESS, it said. Well, that figured. But where was Ralph? Where *was* he? Don't say that he had gone into town!

Maddy was uneasy at being left alone. Despite the comfort of the radio in the kitchen, the house felt very empty and the furniture was strange, larger, almost seemed to be looking at her. She ... her eyes drifted back to the street and she saw what she did not expect to see. Mrs Morgan. It was her, there was no mistaking. She was wearing her usual coat and her black, bat umbrella was arched over her head to keep off the rain. Maddy watched as the woman sailed past, beneath the window.

And then a thought seized her. Possessed her. It grew, itched, burned and would not go away. For WHERE WAS SHE GOING? That was what Maddy wanted to know. To something to do with the book? To something else? Something worse? A hideaway place?

All in an instant, Maddy decided. She marched into the kitchen and took the spare key hanging on the inside door of one of the cupboards, and ran downstairs. Hurrying into her anorak, she closed the front door carefully behind her. It was stealth that was called for—how was she going to follow Mrs Morgan without being seen?

Uncle Alistair reached the cathedral close and there he caught sight of his first people. There were about a dozen of them. Some were sitting on the wet grass, hunched up like savages, with a far-away look in their eyes. One or two were running in circles, whooping and yelling without any purpose whatsoever, while the rest, for some reason, had picked one of the houses beside the choir school and were hurling stones at it. They broke the windows, cheering every time another pane of glass smashed and fell.

Uncle Alistair pressed himself against the wall that edged the pavement, keeping as far away from them as possible, hoping that they would not see him. He waited, summoning his strength, asking. In fact they seem completely absorbed in their own designs and oblivious to anything else. Even to the rain.

He was lucky. They did not see him and he was able to hurry round the corner and on into town. Ralph must have decided to try the supermarket for the milk. There weren't any other shops—open shops—nearby that sold it. The green in front of the cathedral was empty, but he could hear some running and shouting in the distance. And the hubbub of voices.

Maddy followed Mrs Morgan at a discreet distance. The woman was well ahead of her, but unmistakable. She walked in a straight line, turning neither to the left nor to the right, and her feet left no prints on the wet, muddy pavement. Three people were sitting by the side of the road, drenched and bedraggled. They were not talking to each other. Mrs Morgan walked straight past them and not one of them even flinched. It was as if none of them had seen her.

Maddy approached more cautiously. Instinctively she

sensed danger. It flared within her. There was something inside those people, so deep inside that they had never even known it was there. Something like a firework that was ready to go off. Maddy slowed and pressed herself against the garden hedge to pass.

One man turned and snarled. His mouth was wet with the foam of saliva and his eyes were as wide and fierce as a jungle cat's. He lunged at Maddy and yelled, chasing her in a half crouch. His hands trailed in fists below his waist like an ape's. Maddy gave a little scream and tried to push the man away, but he held on to her with one hand and swung the other above his head. She struggled and bit it. With a yelp he drew his arm back quickly, rubbing at Maddy's teeth marks. Then, his face clouding in uncertainty, he crouched down in the gutter again and growled.

Maddy glanced quickly down the street. She had almost lost sight of Mrs Morgan. But no, there she was. Prim and neat, pursuing her unerring course. Turning neither to the right nor to the left. Maddy's arm ached, wrenched at the shoulder. A drop of rain dripped from her nose. Steeling herself inside, she trotted after the disappearing figure of Mrs Morgan. She felt ill, sick, breathless, wet and afraid. But nothing was going to stop her.

The dry fountain in the centre of town was sprinkled with people. Sitting. Just sitting. One woman crawled up its steps on all fours and collapsed in a braying heap.

Uncle Alistair shut his eyes in momentary pain and headed for the supermarket. To see people like this—to see the shape of those evil beasts rampaging inside them—Uncle Alistair shuddered and felt terribly alone. Farther away, a gang of about fifteen youths smashed a chemist's window with planks of wood and then climbed inside. A policeman sat, dazed, on the pavement. And outside the grocer's, a circle of women were searching through one of the big waste bins. There were other people too—zombie-like, sleepwalkers, their memories gone or fuddled, walking with their arms outstretched, stumbling, feeling walls, windows, benches. They did not seem to know where they were or what was happening.

One old man miaowed like a cat and clambered on to a van roof. He lay flat on his belly, his arms and legs splayed, clenching and unclenching his fists.

Uncle Alistair hurried on through the precinct. The supermarket was only a few yards away. On the right. At that moment, without warning, someone flung a fist in his direction and caught him on the jaw. His head swam as he raised his hands in front of his face to protect himself.

Mrs Morgan walked beyond the school and up the hill. The roads were quieter here. Maddy spotted only one woman, cackling insanely in her nightdress. She had climbed on top of a pillar box and was running her hands through her hair. 'It's the end!' she screamed. 'It's the end! The doom has come at last!'

Maddy shuddered and kept on. Straight. Straight behind Mrs Morgan, who had not so much as once looked behind her all this while. 'Where is she going?' thought Maddy. 'Where is she going?'

Uncle Alistair's lip was bleeding and beginning to swell. He had pushed the man to one side with his arm: and the man had stood, snorting like some wild pig, showing his teeth. Uncle Alistair could hardly bear it. Ordinary people. He was very distressed. He nursed his jaw with a gentle, cupped hand and staggered a little past the tailor's and the wallpaper shop to . . .

'Ralph!' he croaked, desperately, the unpleasant iron taste of blood on his tongue. 'Ralph, is that you?'

A shivering little heap in the doorway of the card shop next to the supermarket stirred and looked up. The boy's face was white, white with coal-black holes for eyes.

'Oh, I'm frightened,' he sobbed. 'I'm frightened! Take me home!' he pleaded. 'Please, please, take me home! Away—away from this!'

Around them and on them fell the rain, miserable and relentless, while people, mounds of tattered rags, moved in the filth and the desolation.

Mrs Morgan left the road for Jackson Street, an old row of boarded-up houses that the council were ready to knock down. Work had already begun on one or two of them. It was strange to see inside walls with peeling wallpaper exposed to the air. And fireplaces jutting out over the top of the rubble like some fantastic collage. What had been the road was all cracked and littered now, with green grass growing through it. Windows had been smashed and there was writing on the walls, daubed with white paint and spray cans. It was a depressing place. Its time had gone. Now it was old, dead, empty.

Maddy caught the flash of Mrs Morgan's figure ahead of her. Could this really be the place she was coming to?

Uncle Alistair helped Ralph gently to his feet. 'Come on, we can go now,' he encouraged. 'We'll be safe at home.' Ralph's feet moved slowly, dragging one after the other. He tried not to look at the scene around him, but it was impossible not to. A row of people were stoning the supermarket window and a cheer went up as it finally broke.

'Quickly!' urged Uncle Alistair 'This way!' He hurried Ralph down one of the side streets where there seemed to be nobody about. Ralph was still shaking, his teeth chattering, obviously very shocked. Uncle Alistair for his part was tense, concentrating his mind on the one task uppermost in his thoughts. Getting home.

They came out on one side of the cathedral and, by now, there were more people dotted on the green, pirouetting, yelling, crouched or swaying. Noises escaped from their mouths and polluted the air. Ugly, disgusting. Oinks, screeches and yowls. They were like escapees from some forbidden zoo.

'Oh, Uncle Alistair, can we get past them?' whispered Ralph.

'We'll have to try,' answered Uncle Alistair.

'Can't you make us invisible or something?' asked Ralph.

'Not my style.' He smiled down at Ralph. 'I'm not a magician, you know. Come on.' They hurried forward past the people, who took no notice of them. The cathedral close was in a sorry state, with smashed glass everywhere, but, as yet, no more serious damage. Swiftly, they crossed under the stone arch and back to Ralph's road. There was no one in sight. No one at all.

'I think we're going to be all right,' said Uncle Alistair. 'Maddy's waiting. When we get in, she and I will make you something. Maybe you should have a hot bath.'

Maddy was suddenly conscious of the noise of the falling rain and the hulks of the empty, deserted houses. There was nothing around her. There was nobody. And she had lost Mrs Morgan. All at once. She seemed to have vanished. Turned a corner. Gone into a house. Maddy was not sure. Helpless, she glanced this way and that, not certain whether to go on or back. Suddenly she felt entirely and nakedly alone.

Uncle Alistair opened the front door. Ralph flopped down, his back against the piano and his legs splayed out.

'You can't lie like that, now, Ralph,' scolded Uncle Alistair. 'Get your wet things off. Quickly now!'

Uncle Alistair put his hand on the banister and called from the third step. 'Maddy! Maddy! We're home!'

There was silence. Silence and emptiness.

'That's funny,' he muttered. He ran up a couple of steps. 'Maddy! Maddy! Where are you? Are you there?'

Maddy took one or two cautious steps backwards. She had decided that she did not like this at all. No, not at all. She was just about to retrace her path and run, when a wiry hand caught hold of her wrist and swung her painfully round.

'So, following me, are you? Spying? Well, I have a fit punishment for you!'

'Nnno—nnnoo!' stammered Maddy. Her skin tightened over the whole of her body and her insides turned to ice. It was Mrs Morgan. Her heavy face glowered at the girl and her green eyes were brimming with anger.

'Don't say you weren't following me, because you were! I saw you. My eyes aren't only in the front of my head, you know.'

Maddy gasped and said nothing, because no words would come out. She was held in a strange kind of grip from which she could not free herself, like a rabbit transfixed by a snake. It had happened. The worst thing possible. The worst thing imaginable. She was well and truly caught.

11

The bleak houses stared at Maddy and Mrs Morgan without surprise. Maddy began to sob, but struggled against it, and only a solitary tear trickled down her cheek. Mrs Morgan's fingers tightened cruelly on her arm, and she began to drag Maddy down the deserted street.

Maddy followed meekly for a few steps and then seemed to come to herself: 'No! No!' she yelled, twisting her body and trying to wrench her arm away from Mrs Morgan's grasp. But the woman was set and determined, her face smouldering and malevolent, magnificent but terrible.

'That will do now,' she said quietly in a voice vibrating with menace. 'That will do.' The woman's sharp words brought Maddy up short. Frantically she looked for help, but there was only the empty street with its cracked pavement, rubble and broken glass—and the boarded-up houses. Neglected, blind, forgotten places. Rain fell on their faces, on their shoulders, tin-tacked the puddles and surged in brown spurts out of the drainpipes.

'You'll come with me,' commanded Mrs Morgan. Her voice, her words, were hugely overpowering. They were so strong, so crushing—it was like having your head forced down into a pool of water—all sound cut out, all sound but for those words.

Maddy began to drown.

There was only Mrs Morgan, only Mrs Morgan filling her. Mrs Morgan's words, Mrs Morgan's face, Mrs

Morgan's power, Mrs Morgan's ...

But somewhere, at her back—as if a door, no, a window, was opening—Maddy heard a faint cry. She opened her eyes to see Uncle Alistair's face pressed flat against the glass. And she fancied that she heard the tick, the tick of the grandfather clock, standing so staunch and straight in Ralph's hall. Keeping. Guarding. And she saw the rainbow painted on to it—the rainbow with its promise. A promise of protection, for ever.

'Nnnno—nnno,' she moaned with a whimper, coming round and seeing the street again. 'I won't go with you ... I—I ... won't!'

'Tch!' said Mrs Morgan, chewing the inside of her mouth. With her free hand she took a cigarette out of her coat pocket and lit it with a gold lighter. She inhaled rapidly and breathed out, the smoke billowing into a halo round them both, its smell filtering into Maddy's nostrils. A heavy, swimmy smell, the smell of damp leaves and sad, autumn days, a smell ...

As Maddy's head began to whirl and her vision blurred, a small conscious voice deep within her cried out that she was being drugged.

Uncle Alistair tensed. He had known from the moment he had entered the house that Maddy had gone, but where? Concern overlay his irritation. She should have known. She should have known. The words played over and over again in his mind. But then *something* must have lured Maddy outside, unless, and here he froze suddenly, unless that something had forced its way in. He took off his coat and went upstairs to run a steaming bath for Ralph, still shocked and shaking a little in the hall. The boy's movements were slow as he followed his uncle upstairs like a doll.

'Where are your clothes, Ralph?' asked Uncle Alistair, making each word clear, definite.

'In—in the chest-of-drawers by the window in my bedroom.'

'Fine, now wait just a moment . . .' Uncle Alistair went to look out some fresh clothes for Ralph and came back with neatly folded underclothes, a shirt and a clean pair of trousers. 'Here you are. Go and have a bath . . . you'll feel better . . . But don't fall asleep!'

Ralph mumbled some thanks and took the clothes like a child without speech. He closed the bathroom door behind him and pulled the bolt to.

Uncle Alistair went back into the kitchen and filled the kettle. He banged it down on the cooker and lit the gas. And he made a face. He was worried now, very worried. Outside, in the growing chaos, anything could be happening to Maddy.

'Sit down, dear,' invited Mrs Morgan in a cheerless voice. Maddy obeyed. Her mind felt strapped to a hospital bed, seeing but useless, while her body, for its part, followed all Mrs Morgan's commands. They were inside one of the houses, in what had been the living-room. Light came in between the boards that had been nailed across the broken windows. The walls were damp and peeling. There was an empty fireplace stuffed with old newspapers, a table in the middle of the room, and, scattered across the floor, some old books.

'Now,' continued Mrs Morgan, 'let's see what we have for you, shall we?' She was still puffing at her cigarette. Its smell was so . . . but Mrs Morgan was fussing in a businesslike way. 'Now, ah . . . here we are. This will do. *Animals of the Indian Subcontinent* . . . with pictures. Yes, this will do very nicely.'

Mrs Morgan leafed through the book in a leisurely way, stopping to peer at one or two of the pages. 'This book will keep you company,' she said. 'Only I hope it doesn't turn on you; that would be *too* unfortunate. Now, I must be on my way. Be a good girl and stay here. I'm afraid you will find that you can't do anything else.'

With a quick, unpleasant smile, she was gone. And Maddy was left. For a few moments more her head swam, as if she had fainted or was just waking up after a very real dream. Then suddenly everything around her came into sharp focus—Mrs Morgan, the street, the house, the book. With a start she jerked herself awake. Her head throbbed painfully. She put her hand to her forehead. Then, forcing her legs to stand she glanced around in the gloomy half-light for a door.

There was rain, rain pouring on the roof and on the windows. But the door? She turned, she felt, she looked again and again. Her eyes and fingers searched around the room. It was impossible ... she couldn't break through the windows ... she looked again ... how could there? How could it be? ... and she looked again.

There was no door.

Finally, she squatted down, arms round her knees, in a sobbing heap. She had looked and she had looked. She had searched and she had searched. But wherever she looked and wherever she searched THERE WAS NO DOOR. She was completely and utterly trapped.

Ralph was clean and soap-smelling, his hair flat and shiny. He was definitely more himself. He sat at the kitchen table while Uncle Alistair was frying some eggs.

'But how will we find Maddy?' he asked, knife held upright in his hand. 'I mean, we've got to look for her, even if it does mean going out there again.'

'I know,' replied Uncle Alistair softly. He tried to lift the fried egg out of the pan with a plastic fish slice to stop the yolk bursting. 'I know, but it is difficult. We will have to think how to find her later. Still, I don't think she would have gone out unless there had been a very special reason. Now, eat up—strength and normality are two strong

119

weapons in our hands.'

Ralph ate, munched rather—slowly and thoughtful-ly—thinking to himself and watching his uncle, wonder-ing what was going on inside his head, wondering what he was thinking about. When he had finished, Ralph put his knife and fork to one side and looked down at the yellow mess on his plate.

'What *is* going on?' he asked. 'Why are all the people acting so strangely?'

Uncle Alistair let out a long breath and stood up, drawing with his finger on the formica, 'Let's just say—uh—"Things fall apart; the centre cannot hold" ... let's say ... let's say ... nothing ...'

And, at that moment, unexpectedly and startlingly, the phone rang. Breaking their thoughts. *Brr brr. Brr brr.* The phone rang. It jangled the silence, demanding attention. Ralph looked at his uncle in open amazement while Uncle Alistair merely bowed his head to show an acceptance of the inevitable and went through to the hall to answer it.

Maddy's tears had dried, but she was hungry, wet and uncomfortable—and cold. Her fingers had whitened till they had begun to hurt and her toes had gone to sleep. She banged her feet on the ground to warm them and got up to walk round and round the table. Thoughts, pictures, raced through her head like a film without any meaning, and her breath floated in front of her like a cloud.

'Who was it?' asked Ralph as his uncle put the receiver down.

'Need you ask?' said Uncle Alistair, reappearing in the kitchen.

'Oh,' mouthed Ralph. 'Mrs Morgan. What does she want?'

'She wants me,' replied Uncle Alistair, putting both his hands on the back of one of the kitchen chairs, 'as I thought she would. Well, there is nothing for it.'

'But what?' said Ralph.

'But to go and speak to her,' answered Uncle Alistair.

'You can't!' gasped Ralph. 'She's ...'

'Oh, I know what she is, and she knows that I know. There are, however, one or two things that she doesn't know that I know, and that might help me ...'

'Such as?' asked Ralph.

'Such as what we saw last night and the copies I have of the pages from the spell book. Now I know what she can get up to. Those things. She might have spells, but I have—well, I have ... something else. Something better.'

'But ...'

'No buts. If it has to be done, it has to be done. Besides, meeting her might be a quicker way of finding out where Maddy is.'

Ralph pushed his plate to meet the ketchup bottle, and looked upset. He crossed his arms and stuck out his bottom lip, not in a sulk exactly, but because he felt his uncle was about to do something foolhardy.

'What's the matter with you?' questioned Uncle Alistair suddenly, and with a sigh. 'You don't think ...? Oh, don't worry ... I'm not going in to see her unprotected. That would be foolish in the extreme. No, I shall be protected. And, hopefully, if I'm right, she will not have guessed the kind of protection I shall have.'

'What's that?' muttered Ralph, perhaps a touch sullenly.

'Why,' said Uncle Alistair with a grin, 'it lies with you.'

Maddy put her hand up to one of the boards nailed across the window. She pushed and thumped, but there was no give in it. Then she walked round the room, kicking the books and scattered fragments to one side, trying to see if there was anything she could use as a lever. Anything, anything at all to help her get out. But there was nothing, as Maddy knew there had to be nothing. So she went back to the window and put her cheek to the board, to see what she could see out of the tiny grey crack between it and the wall.

'What do I have to do?' demanded Ralph.

'This,' said Uncle Alistair. 'Now, listen carefully—it's simple, but it's difficult too.' Uncle Alistair ripped a piece of paper off the notebook that Ralph's mother kept fixed to the kitchen wall and began to scrawl on it. Ralph leaned forward in his chair to see what his uncle was doing.

'Now, Ralph,' explained his uncle, finishing writing with a full stop banged onto the page, 'this is a word.' Ralph looked at it. 'But it's not an ordinary word, it's a word of power, like a weapon. It's not a word you'd ever find in any book of spells.' Ralph squinted at the paper. Certainly it was like no other word that he had ever seen. For it did not make sense. Try as he might, Ralph could not actually focus on the whole word from any angle—he could not take it in. All he could do was to concentrate on one letter at a time, but then, the moment that he thought it was fixed in his head, and he shifted his eyes to a new part of the word, he forgot it again. Concentration was useless. He shifted in his chair. He felt queasy, sea-sick.

'That's right,' observed Uncle Alistair, seeing the greenish colour of Ralph's face. 'It does that to you. Now, I'm going out at two—when the clock downstairs strikes. When it strikes half-past, if I'm not back, you must look at the paper, memorize the word, burn the paper, and then say it out loud.'

'But,' said Ralph, his face clouding, 'if I can't read the word now, how will I be able to then?'

'All at the proper time,' said Uncle Alistair. 'You can't run until you can walk—the one thing has to come before the other. Now, half-past two mind. When the clock strikes, and not a moment later. Otherwise ... otherwise all that is at stake may be lost.'

Uncle Alistair hurried into his coat and dashed down-stairs. The mechanism of the grandfather clock was already whirring and, at the stroke of two, he opened the front door and vanished into the falling world outside.

The door shut. Bang. Ralph picked up the piece of paper his uncle had scribbled on and held it to the light. No, it was no good. However hard he tried, he could not read it and, carefully, he put it back on the kitchen table. He sat down in a chair and scraped his heels on the floor, in time with a tune that had darted into his head. But . . . but—the red second-hand on the silent clock by the cooker wheeled round. A slow, interminable round. A minute dragged by. One, just one. There were still another twenty-nine to go.

Maddy rubbed her hands and tried to settle into a comfortable position on the floor of the room. She huddled into a corner between the fireplace and the wall, pulling her hands back into her sleeves and sitting on her feet. She had gone past the point of panic now. She was stuck, and that was that. Stuck with the dirt and the rain and the damp. Wrinkling up her nose, she bent forward till her mouth touched her knee, curling as small as she possibly could, to try to go to sleep.

Ralph, meanwhile, had coiled like a spring. He was distracted. What was happening. What was happening, he wondered? Between Uncle Alistair and Mrs Morgan. What? What? Restless, he went upstairs and began tidying up his room. Anything to make the minutes pass. Then, when he had finished, he wandered round and round the house, continually going back to the kitchen to look at the clock. As he stared at it he willed the limpet-like minutes to fall, to drop away until the hands finally pointed to half-past two. It had taken ages.

Ding-dong, ding-dong.

The grandfather clock in the hall chimed at last and

Ralph gulped, trembling, pent-up and exhausted from all the worry of the previous half-hour. He leaned slowly over the kitchen table and smoothed out the piece of paper. Like a reflection on a pond gradually coming together after the ripples from a stone have disturbed it, so the letters, the very shape of the letters, and the word, seemed to piece themselves together, to come, mingle, form and stare up at Ralph. The word was there, laid bare in front of him, plain and unambiguous.

Ralph spoke it to himself a couple of times under his breath, to make sure that he had it, then picked up the box of matches that his mother used for lighting the gas. He struck one. It went out, smoking. Ralph tutted and struck another. It sparked with a fizz and burned. He lifted the paper between forefinger and thumb and let the fire take to it. The paper blackened and curled at the bottom as the yellow flame rose smoky sheer.

Ralph dropped the paper into the sink and, shoulders hunched almost to his ears, he went through the living-room and stood by the window. With a deep breath he opened his mouth, closed his eyes and—uttered the word.

Oh, the word. That word. Out it came, with an effort, hurting. It did not want to be born into the world. Not that word, for it had not been forged for existence in this world. It was a weapon of another order. It was a weapon of power, a hefty crushing of might. Ralph felt the weight pass from him. His chest lightened and he opened his eyes. He was completely drained and gasping. Wobbly. All he wanted to do was crawl onto the sofa and go to sleep. But, Uncle Alistair. He must see that he was all right.

Down the road a white hand grasped the bars of Mrs Morgan's gate. Clutching his chest, bent almost double, his coat flying, Ralph's uncle reeled out into the street. Ralph gave a start and, without thinking, flew downstairs, leaving the front door open wide. He rushed out onto the road in only his socks. Uncle Alistair appeared to be in some kind of shock, his body rigid and jerking, like some kind of stunned insect.

'Uncle Alistair! Uncle Alistair!' yelled Ralph. 'Are you all right ... are you ...?'

'Ralph? Ralph?' rasped Uncle Alistair. He swallowed hard and pummelled his chest with his fist. 'I'm, I'm sorry ... I can't see you too well.' He was wheezing, his eyes watering, like a blind man fumbling through smoke. 'Quick, quick, we must go in ... we must ...' and an odd sound came from his throat.

'Here!' Ralph put his uncle's arm round his own shoulder and began to half drag him towards his own garden gate. Uncle Alistair's feet were like jelly on the pavement. Down the road one or two people appeared, yelling. One shook a bamboo cane like a spear, another growled.

'Hurry! Hurry!' cried Ralph. He pulled harder at his uncle. There was a shout, and the man with the spear began to run towards them, whooping and lifting the cane like a javelin above his head.

'Uncle Alistair, please ...' said Ralph. 'Oh, please ...' And, with a tug, he managed to pull his uncle half-way up the garden path. For some reason the man with the cane stopped dead at the garden gate, wavered for a moment as though fighting with himself, and then wandered away. The power that Uncle Alistair had called on for protection was obviously still at work.

'That was—that was very close,' stuttered Ralph, helping his uncle into the hall and closing the door behind him. 'What—what happened to you?'

Uncle Alistair sat on the bottom stair with his head in his hands, wheezing. He coughed and cleared his throat, looking out of a pair of bleary, bloodshot eyes at Ralph.

'She's very strong,' he said, more to himself than to Ralph, 'very strong. You were just in time, Ralph, just in time. Well done.'

'And Maddy?'

'Oh, yes, Maddy...' Uncle Alistair stood up in slow, painful stages, like a jointed piece of card unfolding, piece after piece. 'Clues, scraps, but... later... that has to be for later. I'm so tired now... I must... I must go and lie down. Oh, Ralph, you've no idea... I didn't imagine... I couldn't... how could I? I should have... but that's me... I always think I can do everything. I should really rely on what I know.' He coughed and spluttered and swallowed again. racking his lungs and putting the back of his hand across his mouth.

'Oh, dear,' he mumbled to himself, 'I'm not in a very good way.' Each step was a shuffle, an effort, one in front of the other. And, 'I'll be down later, Ralph. You must just make do for now. Leave me for a while.' And, battered, old almost, he climbed the stairs to his bedroom to find some rest.

Maddy stirred in her sleep and mumbled. She was dreaming vague dreams, having found an unsatisfactory but brief respite for her continuing nightmare.

Ralph stretched out on the sofa in the living-room and opened a comic. But it was no good, there was no good in it. All the time he felt the ache of not knowing where Maddy was, of not being sure what had happened to his uncle. His mind was elsewhere. Ralph tried and tried to push back the uncomfortable feeling that the final stages of something were closing in.

12

As Ralph sat, the afternoon ticked by, the rain stopped, and all that was left were the reflections of the clouds glowering in the puddles. Some crazed people passed by the front of the house, but not many. One ragged string of five youths had painted themselves with tiger stripes and came stalking behind the parked cars. But they were soon gone.

Ralph clicked the television on, for something to do, and was astonished to find that there was not one, no, not one news item about what was happening in the town. The air, the surface skin of normality had somehow been maintained. All that was happening was private, hidden, but profound—the awful coming to birth of something hidden deep beneath the skin.

The TV quickly palled. Ralph could not concentrate or relax. Instead, he kept changing his position on the sofa and getting up to wander around the room. He walked out into the hallway and cocked an ear at the stairs. Silence. Uncle Alistair was still asleep. Nothing stirred. Eventually Ralph himself sprawled out on the sofa, tired from the night before, and closed his eyes. He was drowsy and longed for some relief from the worry of all that might be happening to Maddy and all that had happened to his uncle. His eyes blinked and closed slowly, erratically, until he drifted off.

The grandfather clock in the downstairs hall ticked on, measuring out the afternoon. The light outside changed and deepened, the freshness and ripeness of the afternoon calming to prepare for evening. The street of houses was impassive in the aftermath of the rain, its lawns drenched, its pavements splashed with water that had collected into blotches of puddles. The sky was a dull, sunless glow of grey-blue—luminous, unyielding and miserable. Miserable.

The clock downstairs chimed. Ralph rubbed his eyes and awoke, stretching and shrugging. It was five o'clock. The house was still quiet—calm and creaking like a deserted ship, but Ralph decided that he couldn't, just couldn't leave his uncle any longer. He padded into the kitchen and took a can of tomato soup out of the cupboard, warmed it through in a pan and poured some of it into a mug. *St Gregory's* was chiselled beside the handle—it was a mug from school. Then he climbed the stairs with the steaming offering held between his hands.

The bedroom where Uncle Alistair was sleeping was the spare, next to Ralph's parents, and between their room and the bathroom. The door was open and the curtains had been half-pulled together—obviously in a hurry. Uncle Alistair was lying with his head back on the pillow, and resting on his left arm. As Ralph entered in his stockinged feet there was a rustle of blankets from the bed and his uncle rolled over to look at him.

'Oh, Ralph,' he said, 'it's you' (as though it could be anybody else). 'I was awake. Soup—oh, how nice!' He took the mug, sitting up straighter, and began to sip the hot, thick orangey liquid. 'Mmm—that's good,' he said. 'Put the light on.'

Ralph scrambled down on his hands and knees and plugged in the bedside lamp. The butter glow snapped on, filling and changing the room.

'Better?' asked Ralph in a small voice, perching on the end of his uncle's bed.

'Better,' grimaced Uncle Alistair, 'but not well. Well enough, though.'

'What did she do to you?' asked Ralph, finally putting the question that had been plaguing him the whole afternoon.

'Well, she tried to do a lot, but couldn't quite manage it. She managed a bit, though, and then you came along. That held her up enough for me to get out. That, in simple terms, is what happened.'

Ralph realized that he wasn't going to get the complicated terms, so he sat, pulling one of his legs under him on the bed and stretching the other one out straight.

'What about Maddy—did you find out anything about her?'

'Ah, Maddy. That's a difficult one—I found out some scraps, but *she* didn't want to give them away. She's in a house somewhere—I saw a picture of it—it's an old, empty, broken house. That's all—could be anywhere—but we'll have to start looking the moment I'm up. What's the time?'

'It's after five.'

'What?!' Uncle Alistair slumped back and gave a groan. He ran a hand through his hair and let out a deep breath. 'Oh, no! That means we'll have to be double quick. We have two things to do this evening, then.'

'Which are . . .?'

'Find Maddy and stop the witch. Tonight is the night of the full moon, remember. It's tonight that whatever it is that's going to happen will happen. And I found out one thing.'

'What's that?' asked Ralph.

'She definitely plans to destroy the town by water, not by fire.'

Uncle Alistair made a move to get up. His actions were slow and careful, as if he had a weight attached to each of his limbs and had to move them according to the rules of some dance. But he was walking—and moving—though each effort he made was accompanied by a rueful smile.

'I'm so stupid,' he said to Ralph. 'I feel so ill. I should have known the risk I was taking. This is so much my own fault—really, it's ridiculous.' Ralph helped him into his coat.

'Now,' continued Uncle Alistair, 'can you find something that belongs to Maddy—I don't know—a brooch, a hairslide, something like that.'

'I'll see.' Ralph ran across the landing to the little room where Maddy was sleeping. Her pyjamas lay across the bed and there was a scatter of things on the table. Her clothes were springing half-out of the bag she had brought, like stuffing coming out of a cushion. Ralph poked about in the bag and then, on the table, he spied a brooch. It was an old cairngorm one that Maddy's mother had given her, one Maddy liked carrying about with her. She liked its glitter and its shape. Ralph's fingers closed around it and he took it downstairs to his uncle. 'Here,' he said, holding out the ornament.

'Ah, that will do nicely,' said Uncle Alistair, taking it. 'You and I,' he continued, 'are going to be bloodhounds, and we need this to help us find Maddy. Now—do you know where there are any deserted houses?'

Ralph looked helpless and shrugged.

'We'll just have to begin at the beginning, then. My only hope is that Mrs Morgan doesn't take out her anger on Maddy. She wasn't in a very good mood when I left. Now, come on.' Furtively, Uncle Alistair opened the front door. There was no one outside, no one at all. 'All clear,' he whispered. 'We're off!'

Maddy had woken, hungry and damp. She was dismayed to find herself still in the same place. She uncurled and tensed, her eyes heavy and her face drawn, half-ghost in the failing light. The rain had stopped and the only noise was that after-the-event dripping stillness. Then a noise caught her off guard.

Sudden and sharp. Maddy's ears pricked up like a dog's and she immediately became alert and defensive. She shrank further into her corner, unsure of where it had come from. It came again. A flutter and a hiss, like ... Maddy gazed round the room: all that she could still see of it. Every square inch—until—until her eyes rested on the book that Mrs Morgan had left lying on the table. *Animals of the Indian Subcontinent*—with pictures. With pictures ... with ... with ... Maddy gave something between a cry and a squeal and put her hand to her mouth. The thick book on the table was beginning to open, its cover being thrust up. *Something was trying to force its way out of the pages.*

Uncle Alistair and Ralph moved quietly along the street, featureless in the sickly orange light that shone from the lamp posts. It was dark now, late now. Too much time had passed. Too much time had been wasted.

Uncle Alistair would have hurried had he been able. The tide of mad people had either retreated to their homes or gone elsewhere. It seemed as if the roads in this part of the town were bare and belonged to them alone.

'Wait,' puffed Uncle Alistair, slowing and gasping for breath. 'Are you sure you don't know where there are any deserted houses round here?' Ralph shook his head.

'She could be anywhere, then—except the centre of town. It didn't—feel—like the centre of town to me. Somewhere else, somewhere I haven't been before.' Ralph shrugged again.

'Let's try this way, then. One way is as good as another till we find something.' Ralph's uncle pointed up a street (they all looked so alike in the dark) and began to lead the way. Ralph kept up beside him.

There were no people, but, in the distance, Ralph could hear shouts and yells floating over the roofs and the heads of the trees. Then, looking back as they climbed the hill, he spotted the distant flickering flares of bonfires. Orange and menacing, like creatures daring the night.

The houses were bigger at the top of the hill and detached from each other. Uncle Alistair took Maddy's brooch out of his pocket and held it flat in the palm of his hand, like a compass. He moved round in a full circle, then stopped.

'Nothing yet,' he explained. He looked a little downcast. 'We must be in completely the wrong place.'

Maddy stood up, her knees still sagging, and pressed back against the crumbly wall. For, out of the pages of the book, had nudged a lizardy head with a flicking tongue and steady bead-like eyes. It twisted and hissed, its long tongue greedy and much in evidence. It was pulling and pulling, with some difficulty, pulling itself into birth from the pages of the book. It advanced steadily, tugging and tugging.

Maddy saw the wide, brilliant flaps on each side of its neck, patterned and entrancing. In bright colours. She was sure she knew what it was. It must be a cobra. Maddy could see that now. One of the most deadly snakes of all—but different too, for it glowed phosphorescently in the gloom, red and bright white-green. Maddy's hands changed to a sick colour in the blackened room.

But Maddy did not scream or panic. Instead, with ice-cold calculation, her brain working overtime, she eased herself back into a sitting position, as cautiously as she could, trying not to attract the creature's attention. 'Uncle Alistair!' she thought. 'Ralph! Where are you now?'

Something pulsed in Uncle Alistair's pocket. It was the brooch. Maddy's brooch. He held it in his cupped hand and moved it about in front of him. It jerked his arm, as if some kind of electricity were suddenly passing through it.

'At last, Ralph,' he breathed. 'This is what we want.

Down here.' And he began to hurry off. His long coat hung below his knees and his feet clattered on the pavement. Ralph followed behind and together their footsteps echoed in an odd harmony, bouncing off the walls of the houses on either side of the street. They walked down three or four streets at a brisk pace until they came to a crossroads with traffic lights and shops opposite.

'Listen!' warned Uncle Alistair, stopping abruptly and holding a forefinger up in the air. 'Move quietly.' He and Ralph edged further down the street and flattened themselves against the wall of a house that stood sideways on to the road. Peering round, they saw that a bonfire had been stacked up in the middle of the street and set alight. Chairs, tables, sofas, boxes and other furniture had been piled up in an uneven tower and set fire to. Smoke belched from the flames up into the sky. About twenty people stood around, some crouching, one or two on all fours. Most were staring, however, as though hypnotized, and chanting something that neither Ralph nor his uncle could hear.

'We'll have to go the other way round,' whispered Uncle Alistair. 'Back off quietly.'

Ralph's uncle took the boy's hand and pulled him away, further down the road, until the noise and the flames were well behind them.

The snake's head was now arched over the table and, in a long, sinuous curve, had reached the floor. Maddy stared and wondered how much more of it there was to come out. It hissed, hostile and malevolent. Its coils oozed out behind it. More and more, spilling out onto the table and dropping onto the floor.

Maddy's mouth opened, dry and soundless, as the snake's head positioned itself at the foot of the table. Unerringly, its eyes swivelled slowly round to fix themselves on her. It hissed and began to lift itself up.

Maddy pressed herself even further back, but there was nowhere else to go. She dreaded the thing touching her, but it was by now so big that she did not see any way of preventing it from doing exactly what it wanted to.

'We must be closer by now,' said Uncle Alistair. 'Look!' The brooch was shaking in his hand and right up his arm. 'What's along there?' He pointed down a dark street.

'I don't know,' replied Ralph, feeling lamer each time he answered his uncle. 'I don't come up here much.'

'Well, it can't be helped,' said Uncle Alistair. 'Outwards—alongwards. We can't have far to go now.'

They had walked such a distance from Ralph's house since they had set out, and through such a maze of streets, that Ralph had all but lost his way. He only hoped that his uncle knew what he was doing.

Maddy felt her strength going, being drawn somehow into the figure of the snake. A helplessness seized her as her limbs collapsed one by one. She half toppled, falling like a wax doll onto the floor while the snake, with precise cunning and movement, looped its head around her right leg and began to pull tight. It began to pull tight.

Uncle Alistair stopped at a hole in a broken fence that led off the road. 'This must be the place,' he pronounced. They had finally reached the outskirts of the deserted block of houses. There were no lamp posts here, or cars, or curtains, or any kind of human life at all. Uncle Alistair clenched the brooch tightly in his fist for a moment and shook it with a sudden movement to calm it. With that it became no more than a brooch again and ceased moving. He popped it back into his pocket and put a hand to either side of his mouth.

'Hallooo!' he called down the echoey waste. 'Maddy!

134

Maddy! Can you hear me?'

The snake began to coil round Maddy's other leg and then rested its head for a moment on her tummy. She felt its weight and its slithering, its noise and its glow—but there was nothing, nothing that she could do. She was completely paralysed.

'Maddy!' called Uncle Alistair again. 'Maddy, you must be around here somewhere!' He walked briskly past the hulks of each of the houses. His feet splashed in the puddles. Ralph tagged behind, afraid of losing sight of his uncle in such a treacherous and unpredictable place. 'Maddy? Maddy?' Uncle Alistair's voice was insistent.

Maddy. That was it. Maddy. That was the word. Maddy. *Her name.* That was it. *Her name that was.* Maddy. Maddy.

She screamed, a dam-burst of a noise. Her whole self concentrated into the one space that was her mouth.

She screamed, and the noise raced like wildfire down the ramshackle street. It was an alarm that set Uncle Alistair's and Ralph's ears ringing. She screamed and she screamed and then stopped, gasping, her mouth wet with her own saliva.

'Oh, Ralph, Ralph!' muttered Uncle Alistair, gaining speed. His long legs moved as fast as they were able. Faster they moved past house after house after house, until: 'In here, Ralph!'

Ralph's uncle pushed open the half-hinged front door of the house where Maddy was and rushed inside. He waded through dust and fallen plaster, into what had been the living-room. In through the door. Maddy was lying sobbing on the floor. Uncle Alistair bent down to pick her up while Ralph hovered, unsure of what to do, in the doorway.

'What—what?' soothed Uncle Alistair as gently as he could. 'Is it all right?'

'The—the snake...' stuttered Maddy, choking and breaking on her sob. 'There was a snake. It was here... it was...'

'Just... just a minute,' calmed Uncle Alistair. 'It's all right now. We've all, all three of us had a very rough ride today. Shh. It's all right now.'

He helped Maddy to her feet and she stood, dumb and confused. Ralph switched his torch on and the beam of light brought to life all the corners of the room.

'But—but there wasn't a door!' she exclaimed. 'I looked and looked, and there wasn't a door.'

'Then what happened?' asked Uncle Alistair softly. 'How did you get here?'

'I—I followed her—Mrs Morgan—and she caught me and put me in here. But there wasn't a door.'

'And then?'

'Then I waited and—and—a snake came out of that book—on the table and—it was really horrible.' Maddy put her hands to her face and began crying again, exhausting her body with deep sobs.

Ralph picked his way over to the table and shone the torch on the book. *Animals of the Indian Subcontinent* it said on the title. With pictures. Ralph opened the cover and began turning over the pages. 'That's funny,' he said, after a few minutes.

'What?' asked Uncle Alistair sharply.

'The photograph of the cobra—in the book. It's blank!'

'Let's leave this place. Now!' declared Uncle Alistair with a shudder. 'Whatever black thing was happening here—it's over!'

Without another word he led Ralph and Maddy out into the night.

They walked back, the three of them abreast, avoiding the main streets and sticking to quieter places. The journey home was swifter, as they knew where they were going and, apart from having to keep an ear and an eye open for any stray people they might happen to come across, they felt more at ease. It was a long walk back. There were walls and gardens and houses, and lollipop lamp posts lit the way. Finally, with immense relief, they found themselves once again in Ralph's road, and then they were safe at last in the confines of the house.

But it was late.

'Another can of that soup all round, Ralph,' suggested his uncle. 'We need something inside us before we go out again.'

'Out *again*?' groaned Maddy.

'Yes, it's the full moon tonight, remember. We must be there.'

'Where?' asked Maddy.

'Good question,' replied Uncle Alistair, 'a very good question indeed.'

Ralph poured the soup into bowls and put three spoons on the table—then gushed cold water from the tap into the empty soup pan. He took a quick look out of the window, holding the curtain back for a moment. 'It's clearing,' he said. And it was.

Outside, the clouds were edged with light, massive and parting, revealing the black of the sky beyond. And the moon. The moon, fuzzy, appeared suddenly from behind a cloud, shedding its radiant light. Only for a moment, and then it ducked behind another cloud.

'Soon the sky will clear, and then she will begin.'

'But where?' said Ralph. 'Where?'

Maddy yawned and unfolded the newspaper that was lying on the chair next to her. It was the one with Mrs Keensby's dragon in it, and the headline . . .

'Water,' repeated Uncle Alistair, half musing, 'destruction by water . . .'

And the headline, on the newspaper, that had been there all the time: FREWIN DAM NEARS COMPLETION.

'Destruction by water,' said Ralph again. 'But how?'

'Oh, goodness!' exclaimed Maddy suddenly, dropping her spoon into her soup.

'What's the matter?' asked Uncle Alistair.

'The dam—the Frewin Dam! *That's* how she's going to destroy the town! She's going to burst the dam! That's what the water monster's for!'

'You're right!' shouted Uncle Alistair, leaping to his feet. 'You're exactly right. How do we . . .?'

But at that moment he was cut short. For a roar filled the night, shaking the trees and the houses to their roots. Such a roar it was, primal and uncompromising, the very substance of terror brought horribly to life.

'What—what's the time?' demanded Uncle Alistair, turning suddenly ashen.

'Well—what is it?' Urgency and panic were swelling in his voice. But there was no need for either Maddy or Ralph to answer. For, from downstairs, came the chimes of the grandfather clock and the count of twelve.

It was midnight.

'That's—that's impossible!' gasped Uncle Alistair, seizing the back of one of the kitchen chairs with both hands and gripping it tight. 'That's simply impossible! It can't be twelve yet!'

And all at once the house shuddered, a deep shaking that came from the very bowels of the earth itself. The trees outside went mad. Lights came on in all the houses.

'She's tricked us!' declared Uncle Alistair. 'She's tricked us!'

'But—but,' trembled Maddy, 'how—how? Does that mean she's won?'

There was a creaking and a drunken tipping, and above them a crack appeared right across the kitchen ceiling. Another roar tore at the heart of the night. They all felt it. They all felt its weight and the pull of its power.

'Is—is this the end, then?' ventured Ralph, hardly daring to speak. 'Are we really too late?'

'Perhaps,' breathed Uncle Alistair, still gripping the chair, his eyes fixed on the space ahead of him, 'perhaps, after all, we are.'

Maybe it was Maddy's imagination, but, as the long, bellowing roar began to rumble and die away, she thought she heard the cackle of triumphant laughter borne in through the kitchen window on the back of the silvery moonlight.

13

The house shook violently and, upstairs, books fell on to the floor.

'Downstairs!' shouted Uncle Alistair, as the cups and plates and forks and knives began to slide along the kitchen table—to clatter and smash on the floor.

Maddy and Ralph ran out and held tight to the banister in the hall. The house seemed to be heaving like a rogue fairground ride gone wildly out of control.

A picture fell off the wall and, gradually, the furniture began to dislodge and move.

Pyoing! Pyoing! Phut! Upstairs, one, two, three light bulbs blew, exploding into darkness, scattering jagged pieces of hot, sharp glass onto the carpet.

And the carpet. Worse the carpet. The whorls and flowers in the carpet began to swirl, seized with a kind of madness. Green shoots and leaves pushed their heads out of the wool and began to twine round the banister and up the wall. Flowers opened, releasing a sticky, sweet, strong-smelling perfume. Flowers with eyes and mouths. Flowers with hands. Flowers with nails. Flowers that could pick humans!

Reflections crowded into the mirrors, queuing to fight free from the other side. They banged the glass with their fists. Reflections with no eyes and blank faces. Reflections that could creep into you when you weren't looking and begin to hack out from the inside.

Clothes drew themselves together in the bedrooms and raised themselves up to dance in a grotesque, frenzied group ... while eyes opened in the wallpaper. Eyes without lids. Eyes that stared. Eyes that could suck you in, like a fly into a furnace, like a rabbit drawn by a snake's unyielding stare.

A book grew a pair of legs and began to walk.

Bedclothes shivered on the bed.

The table in the hall sprouted fur and a wide mouth opened in one of the drawers.

Upstairs, in Ralph's parents' bedroom, the mirror gave way, bending and undulating like the surface of a calm lake that has suddenly been disturbed. Legs and arms and faces began to push their way out.

In the downstairs hall, Maddy gave a yell. For suddenly the floorboards had become red hot and her left leg had begun to sink as if into quicksand.

Ralph put both his hands over his ears and screwed up his eyes tight ... while the piano began to play. Harsh crashing music. Like laughter. Like the triumphant laughter of a woman. Like Mrs Morgan.

'Wait! Wait!' thumped Uncle Alistair, shaking Ralph by the shoulders and helping Maddy pull her leg out of the floor. 'Don't let go! Whatever you do, don't let go!'

Outside, a long, snaky, crumbling crevice opened in the street, a crack that stretched from one end of the road to the other.

'We're not done for yet!' yelled Uncle Alistair. He waved his arms desperately in front of him, a tired swimmer on the home strait, and felt blindly for the glass face of the grandfather clock. Its tick was all but submerged by the shaking and confusion erupting around it. Then it was drowned once more by another almighty roar that shook the night.

Uncle Alistair was breathing heavily, holding on to the clock. He held on as if in a shipwreck, clutching his last possession as the storm raged. And then, with trembling hands, he prised open the face. The rainbow was there still.

141

The rainbow. The rainbow. The promise... of protection... for ever.

Uncle Alistair swallowed hard. Ralph and Maddy had both fallen over, Ralph with his head burrowed into his arms.

'Tonight!' cried Uncle Alistair, seizing the hands of the clock. 'Tonight will just have to be the night that the clocks go back!' And, with a mighty heave, he began to push back the hands of the clock.

Sweat stood out in great drops on his brow and the muscles in his arms ached, painful and throbbing.

Back he pushed the hands, till tears came into his eyes with the effort.

Back, back for a whole hour, until it was impossible to move the clock hands any further.

The moment the long hand touched the twelve mark and the clock showed eleven again, Uncle Alistair fell back gasping, slumping down on the floor and nursing his poor arms. 'Phew!' he sweated. 'That was close!'

Maddy and Ralph both sat up, bewildered. For everything had stopped. Only... it was not quite that everything had stopped, more that it had never even begun.

The clothes, the books and the furniture were back in their proper places—the light bulbs shone as though nothing had arrived to disturb them and the flowers in the carpet were no more than just a pattern of wool again.

'I don't understand,' gasped Maddy. 'How did you do that? It was... It was...'

'Don't say magic,' interrupted Uncle Alistair hurriedly. 'It was necessity. We all may be given the power to do these things from time to time. All that's happened is that it's eleven o'clock now instead of twelve. We have an hour. At twelve all those same things will start happening over again unless we can find Mrs Morgan and stop her.'

Maddy swallowed hard. No more snakes, she hoped.

Only what she had just seen or *thought* she had just seen, had been worse. Far, far worse. Ralph was still blinking and then, half-consciously, asked: 'But how will we get to the Frewin Dam? It's too far to walk, even in an hour.'

'We shall have to borrow a car,' stated Uncle Alistair. 'I'm sure no one would mind if they knew what we were up to!' He opened the front door and bundled both of them out.

Uncle Alistair walked out to the pavement with Maddy and Ralph following behind. The street was quiet, with smashed glass and brick lying everywhere. There was no one around. Uncle Alistair's eyes scanned up and down in the dark. A few houses away a car had been driven up against a lampost. Its headlights were on and a door drooped open. 'We'll take that one,' Uncle Alistair said. He got in quickly and opened the back door for Maddy and Ralph. 'Just a minute,' he said, 'there isn't a key.' He lifted the bonnet and rummaged around in the engine until it coughed and spluttered into action.

'We're off!' declared Uncle Alistair, with brightness in his voice. 'At last. Now, who knows the way to Frewin Dam?'

Maddy knew the way better than Ralph and so she sat in the front of the car beside Uncle Alistair and pointed the way. The car nosed through the quiet streets of the town and then along country lanes, climbing steadily all the while. At one point the car headlights caught a signpost to Frewin in their white stare, and after that it was easy.

'Where's the dam?' asked Uncle Alistair.

'It's up—it's up—there!' said Maddy thoughtfully, indicating a mound of trees. 'There's a car park. That's where we went with the school. You remember, don't you, Ralph?'

Ralph nodded. Uncle Alistair slowed the car and stopped, keeping the engine running.

'Aren't we going all the way up?' asked Maddy.

'What, and announce our arrival with trumpets?' retorted Uncle Alistair. 'No fear. We've got to be as quiet as possible—and—you two have to keep out of sight. Out of sight, out of mind, remember—even if she does have eyes in the back of her head.'

Maddy shuddered at this, remembering all too clearly that she certainly seemed to.

They climbed out of the car and stood for a moment in the whistly darkness. The road turned a bend, and the dam complex was only a few minutes away by foot.

'Come on, then,' waved Uncle Alistair, 'we'd better go and find her. Keep to the side.'

They followed the road to the bend, and then trudged along the border of wet grass under the shielding branches of the trees. Ahead of them was a barrier, a bit like a barber's pole, right across the road, and a hut where a guard normally sat.

Tonight there was no one, but the floodlights were on, bathing the whole of the area in a strong, artificial glare. Steps led down to the offices, still lit, but with their venetian blinds drawn down. The top of the newly completed dam was fitted with a walkway and handrail that spanned it like a small road.

'She's bound to see us the moment we walk into the light,' whispered Ralph, tugging his uncle's sleeve to make him lower his head.

'Perhaps,' conceded Uncle Alistair. 'It depends where she is. Shhh!' He waited, spreading his arms out in front of Ralph and Maddy to hold them back—and then, with a sombre but definite nod of the head, he signalled them to move forwards.

They skirted the barrier and drew closer to the edge of the dam. Ralph cast his eyes along the bright walkway and there, just in sight, was a figure about half-way along, clasping something to her chest. Ralph couldn't really see

144

from where he was standing, but he was sure it was Mrs Morgan.

'Stay here, now!' commanded Uncle Alistair, with a strong movement of the hand.

'Oh, *no!*' protested Ralph. He was frightened, it was true, but he wanted to see what was going to happen. He and Maddy hung back, unwillingly, watching as Uncle Alistair moved nearer and nearer the rapt female figure. She did not appear to have noticed that there was anybody else there.

Ralph chewed the inside of his mouth and spoke into Maddy's ear: 'Look, we've come this far,' he said. 'We *must* see what they're going to do.'

Maddy nodded in agreement. Cautiously, in single file, they began unobtrusively to make their way to where Uncle Alistair and the woman were standing.

Mrs Morgan turned her head smoothly to greet Uncle Alistair. She smiled, half-greeting, half-mocking. Triumphant. 'I did not expect you,' she said, after the pause of a moment.

'I know,' replied Uncle Alistair in a low voice.

Mrs Morgan raised her eyebrows. She was young this evening and irresistibly beautiful. She had put on her best. The book that she had, held close to her chest, was the book of spells.

'Even though you are here, you are too late to do anything to stop me. Things have gone too far.'

'Things have not gone too far yet.'

Mrs Morgan shook her head. 'Poor fool,' she muttered, 'your kind are all the same.' Then, with a quick movement, she stretched out her hand, palm flat, and uttered a long string of words. As she finished there was an answering rumble and the surface of the velvet water far below churned. Big bubbles rose sloppily to the smooth surface and broke.

Uncle Alistair made a move. He lunged forward. But

Mrs Morgan threw a glance at him, like a blinding fork of lightning, and his legs crumpled beneath him. 'Oh!' he gasped.

'That is only an inkling of how strong I have become!' she warned. 'Too strong for you. Too strong for anyone!'

'But why?' Uncle Alistair pleaded. 'Why all this? All those people...'

'Because triumph, power, is all that I want now. What you call evil has become my good. These... people... as you call them,' and she mouthed the word with some distaste, 'think they are good. Good!' she laughed. 'But, with this...' and here she put her hand into the pocket of her jacket, 'with this I will show them. With this, they will know fear. At last, after all these long years, vengeance will be mine!' She pulled the diamond egg from her pocket. The egg from the night on Pig's Hill. She held it out to Uncle Alistair, still cradling the book in her other hand.

'The leviathan will let loose the forces of chaos and then the whole town will die in the destruction of the dam.'

'No!' yelled Uncle Alistair, taking a plunge forward, but unable to move either of his legs.

Mrs Morgan threw her head back. Her skin was almost like alabaster in the artificial light. Still looking Uncle Alistair full in the face, she lifted the egg above her head and tossed it into the water. There was not even the sound of a distant splash as it fell in.

Uncle Alistair's head spun. Mrs Morgan gazed at him in triumph. Ralph and Maddy clutched at the handrail and stared down, down into the water.

Beneath them, something shook. Long strings, snakes of phosphorescent light, began to glow, drawing themselves through the depths of the water to concentrate in one single point. Far below them, two eyes opened, heavy-lidded, startled and still full of sleep. A tail threshed dully. There was a sound. Dart of a long body. The surface of the water shook and then, with an almighty crash and a splash, broke.

Something huge lifted out of the water, dripping green and shaking with fins. Something with eyes as old as time itself. The creature threw back its head and roared.

The rail trembled under their hands. There was a deep vibration beneath their feet. The nightmare was beginning again.

'No!' said Ralph resolutely, shaking the rail and staring at Maddy with wide eyes, 'I'm not going to let it happen again. No! No!' and he ran forward to where Uncle Alistair was kneeling.

As he approached, he could see that Mrs Morgan was beginning to change. Lights played on her face. Her form began to melt and shift, like wax or light; her features, soft as the sand on the shore, fell this way and that, parting like curtains to reveal what was truly within.

Ralph rushed forward and pushed her hard in the chest with all his strength. Surprise showed for an instant on her face as she fell backwards, dropping the book. Ralph scooped it up and hugged it to him. He took a few steps back.

'You ... you ...' she growled, trying to snare him with her eyes. But Ralph knew better than to look at her.

'It's too late now, anyway,' she said, her voice hardening into a rasping croak. 'You're all done for! It's all over! It's the doom!'

Ralph sagged with dismay as the woman picked herself up and began to move towards him. Her arms spread wide in front of her like the paws of a cat. But Ralph dodged back. Below him, with much splashing, the head of the monster writhed in the water. Another bellow rippled through the stillness, just as Ralph backed up to the rail at the edge of the dam. Mrs Morgan slid nearer.

'I've got you now!' she crooned. 'I have. You can't escape me now!' But she swiped empty air as Ralph ducked and led her a dance, further out to the middle of the dam. Panting, the woman advanced, cutting the air with her sharp nails.

'Aiieeee!' she screamed, swooping on Ralph, but he jumped back again. In rage she lifted both hands above her head as though she were going to throw something at the boy... When, with a roar, the loathsome head of the creature appeared above the edge of the dam. Its eyes rolled in its head and foam dripped from its mouth. Its jaws opened wide to let out another trembling, ear-splitting roar... When, with one thought, or with no thought— Ralph did not know why—he took aim and threw the book straight into the jaws of the creature. It vanished, swallowed in one gulp.

Mrs Morgan froze, unnerved, and an expression of pure hate spread across her face.

'It's not too late, you see,' gasped Uncle Alistair from where he was kneeling. All at once he felt the strength begin to flow back into his legs. 'It's not! You who thought to destroy others have now destroyed yourself.'

The monster shook, churning the water, throwing its head back on itself. It coiled, threshing, snarling, shaking from within—turning to shadow, losing its substance, shrinking—dwindling to nothing. Nothing. With a note that was more of a mournful bellow, the creature sank once more beneath the surface of the water and did not rise again.

Mrs Morgan tore at her hair in rage and leaned out over the rail.

'Nooo!' she screamed. 'Nnnooooo!'

But all she heard was her empty rage echoing back at her. She snarled, showing her teeth, and spitting like a big cat, as she slunk back.

'Now,' said Uncle Alistair calmly, extending his hand,

'it's all over. Now, now . . .'

'No!' she growled through teeth gritted tight. She let out a defeated roar and a heavy, pungent animal smell began to fill their nostrils. Maddy felt sick, all of a sudden, and put her hand to her nose. Still working her mouth in a silent fury, Mrs Morgan clambered up onto the handrail of the dam and sat with her legs dangling over the side.

Uncle Alistair blenched and jumped forward. But it was too late. She had already gone, dropped into the water, down into the darkness, like a stone. It was indeed all over.

Maddy gulped and rushed to the edge. Ralph peered over, but neither of them could see anything. There was just the dam and the lights and the trees and the sky and the darkness.

Safe.

Uncle Alistair closed his eyes in relief. 'Well,' was all he said, 'it's over and she's gone. We're safe.'

Ralph shook his head in bewilderment, and Maddy felt tears fill her eyes. Both of them were too tired, too overcome, to register anything more for the moment.

'We can go home now,' announced Uncle Alistair. 'And, what's more—we know we'll find it there when we get there!' He smiled and put his arms round their shoulders.

'Has she—has she really gone?' asked Maddy, anxious to be sure.

'For a long time, perhaps for ever,' answered Uncle Alistair. 'This was a battle, not a war. But—don't worry about that now. Remember the rainbow—the promise, the protection. There will be no flood—no destruction. No matter how great Mrs Morgan's power appears, there are some things she cannot do—and some things she cannot try to do again. Her knowledge is deep, but there are deeper things still that her and her like are blind to.'

Far away, on a distant tree in the wood, a large crow

flapped to rest. Its sharp eyes were two unnerving sparks of green in the night. It opened its beak and let out an ugly croak. Then it flew away.

'Home, home!' sang Uncle Alistair cheerily, leading Maddy and Ralph back to the car. 'Home, home—and—bed!'

14

It was a fresh, sunny morning and washing was blowing like flags in the gardens along the street. The blotches of wet on the pavement were drying up and brilliant, white clouds raced high in the sky. Ralph dozed, lying on his back, his mouth open, in the cloistered gloom of his bedroom.

Brring brring. Brring brring. It was the phone, wakening the house to answer it. Maddy yawned and murmured in the next room, turning over in bed, while Uncle Alistair, who had already brought in the milk from the doorstep, was busy in the kitchen. Ralph heard snatches of his uncle's voice floating up the stairs.

'Oh—oh, hello! Yes, yes, fine. I know. Terrible business. Really? I think so. Wait a minute—Ralph? Ralph!'

Ralph climbed unwillingly out of bed, tousled and sleepy in his stripy pyjamas.

'Who is it?' he called from the top of the stairs.

'Your mother!' shouted Uncle Alistair. 'Come and speak to her.'

Ralph blinked and tried to shake some more of the sleep out of his head. He tottered down to the phone.

'Oh, there you are!' said his mother's voice. There were all kinds of noises behind her and she was indistinct and metallic.

'Where are you?' asked Ralph.

'You'll never guess! I'm at Reading station.'

'Mmm?' said Ralph, scratching the back of his leg.

'Yes, I took the overnight train to London last night.

Granny's much better and I thought I'd come home. Your father and the twins are coming back this evening, too. That means we can all have Easter together.'

'But—wasn't there something wrong with the railway line?' asked Ralph.

'No,' replied his mother in a puzzled voice. 'But I have been reading about what's been happening in the paper this morning. People fainting, and dancing in the streets. I'm glad you don't seem to have been affected. I hear the bishop and the mayor are back on their feet, so everything is in working order again. Still, I suppose you thought it was fun.' *Pip pip pip pip pip pip pip pip.* 'That's it! I have to go! Bye!' *Brrrrrrrrrrrrrrrr.* Ralph put the receiver down.

'You have five minutes till breakfast,' yelled Uncle Alistair from the kitchen. 'Will you go and get Maddy up?'

'Sure,' nodded Ralph, and he began the trek up the carpeted stairs to the bathroom.

Washed and clean—well, as washed and clean as usual—Ralph made his appearance at the breakfast table, followed by Maddy, who seemed still half asleep.

'There's no time for yawning,' said Uncle Alistair. 'We have a lot to do.'

'Like?' asked Ralph.

'Phone Maddy's mother for one thing. I'm sure she'll be ready to come home now, and then we have to go and collect your mother from the station at half-past ten. I've looked at the timetable, and I should be able to catch a London train at the same time.'

'You mean, you're going!' spluttered Ralph, gulping down a big mouthful of his cereal.

'I think it's about time,' answered Uncle Alistair smoothly. 'I've been here long enough. Besides, uncles are only for adventures, you know—and the adventures seem well and truly and thankfully over for the present.'

Maddy spooned some sugar into her coffee and spread a slice of toast with marmalade.

'And what did Mum mean about the paper—reading about people fainting, and dancing?'

Uncle Alistair smiled. 'One thing you will learn,' he said, 'is that people always have to have an explanation for everything, especially the things they can't account for very well. Here, look at this!' and he tossed Ralph the morning paper which had been stuck through the letter-box just as usual.

On the front page there was a big black-and-white photograph, with the headline in giant print: CHEMICAL LEAK CAUSES CHAOS.

'It seems,' continued Uncle Alistair drily, that a chemical leak into the local water supply after that big storm was the cause of all the illness, depression and scenes of madness that we were witness to. That's one reason why none of this appeared in the papers sooner. Government experts needed time to investigate: so they put a news ban on the whole story.'

'But . . .' said Maddy.

'But what?' asked Uncle Alistair, opening his eyes mock-wide.

'That's not what really happened.'

Uncle Alistair smiled and then looked sombre. 'It's often very difficult to find out what *really* happened. But in this case, as far as everyone is concerned, the story in the newspapers is the true one, and anything you say will be dismissed as mere fantasy.'

'Then we can't tell anyone!' exclaimed Ralph.

'You can tell each other,' said Uncle Alistair. 'That's something. Many people walk round the world with stories locked inside them, truths that they are unable to tell anybody. That is the way of things. Only, there comes a time when you *can* tell the truth, and when that happens it will come out all the more powerfully and really make a difference! But I must go and pack.'

Uncle Alistair disappeared to his room, leaving Maddy

153

and Ralph to tidy away the breakfast things and do the washing up. When he returned downstairs the kitchen was clean and he was in his best dark suit and tie, with a small, battered suitcase in his right hand. Before they set out, they rang the hospital. Maddy's mother was delighted.

'Maddy!' she shouted brightly, crackling down the line. 'The phones have been out of order your way and I read in the papers this morning what an awful time you've all been having. I'm so glad you're all right. They're letting me home this afternoon, so I'll see you then. Bye.'

'Everything all right? asked Uncle Alistair.

'Yes,' nodded Maddy, a little dazed, 'she's coming home later today.'

'Brilliant!' beamed Uncle Alistair.

Ralph, Maddy and Uncle Alistair walked through the fresh breezy streets to the station. It was about twenty minutes from Ralph's house. Women with prams were back in the streets, old men and women, and the bikers and those not at school. The broken glass had all been swept up and the boarded windows and overturned cars were the only tell-tale signs of all that had happened. The cathedral close was tranquil as ever, while the High Street thronged with shoppers. All with their eyes on their bags and their children. All talking about the dreadful last few days.

The station was a small one, fronted by a car park lined with rows of gleaming vehicles. Uncle Alistair went to buy his ticket and then came back.

'You stay here,' he said. 'Your mother's train will be in in a minute—and so will mine, on the other side.'

He smiled and put an affectionate arm round their shoulders. But he was still distant somehow. Ralph reflected that even if you had him for a hundred years, it would never be possible to know the whole of Uncle

Alistair. He clattered nimbly down the steps of the underpass, leaving Ralph and Maddy to pass by the ticket collector onto the wide platform and wait for the incoming train. Uncle Alistair appeared on the other side of the track and put down his suitcase beside him on the platform. They all put their hands to their mouths and yelled across the space.

'I think I left my alarm clock!' shouted Uncle Alistair. 'Will you send it to me?'

'Yes!' shouted Ralph.

'Here's my train!' shouted Uncle Alistair, indicating down the track. 'Goodbye! Goodbye!' and he took the rolled-up morning newspaper out of his coat pocket and waved farewell to Maddy and Ralph as the engine rolled into the station. At that moment he was lost to view.

'Goodbye! Goodbye!' they yelled, as the train from Reading drew to a slow halt in front of them. Doors opened all along and people began to climb out of the train. Men in business suits, mothers with children and grannies on a visit, and: 'Ralph! Maddy! There you are!' It was Ralph's mother, curly-haired, smiling and carrying a travelling bag. 'What a crowd! The train was terribly busy.'

A queue formed to show their tickets and, with a jerk, and a roar, the train from Reading and Uncle Alistair's train pulled out of the station in different directions.

'At least it's a nice day,' observed Ralph's mother. 'You and Maddy will be able to go outside. For, if there's one thing that's certain, I know that I'll have to clean the house from top to bottom after my brother's been in it.'

She laughed. 'He's a terrible man. He could have waited. At least till after lunch.'

Ralph twisted round to the bare track behind him and looked over to the other platform. The London train had gone and now the flat, grey expanse was quite, quite empty. He felt downcast.

'I don't see why he had to go so quickly,' he mumbled to Maddy.

'Maybe he's got something else to do—somewhere else,' suggested Maddy.

'But what are we going to do today, it's . . .'

'Wait,' said Maddy, shaking Ralph's arm. 'I want to go round today and look at everything and touch it and know it's real and there. All the things we see every day and don't notice. I really want to. It's important.'

'Oh, well,' said Ralph, agreeing unwillingly, 'we can do that, I suppose.' He glanced back at the empty platform once again, for the last time, as they passed the ticket collector.

'Oh, Ralph,' chided Maddy, 'your uncle can't be here all the time, but don't tell me that he ever really goes away.'

Ralph sighed and made a face.

'But it's still true what he said,' continued Maddy, as they walked out to the car park, Ralph's mother one or two steps ahead. The sun shone on the windows of the buildings while snowy gulls wheeled in the air, crying to each other. A red double decker bus stopped in front of the traffic lights and a dog licked at a fallen ice-cream cone.

'I think we'll get a taxi home as it's a special occasion,' declared Ralph's mother, walking over to the rank. 'I'm too tired to walk.'

'What did Uncle Alistair say, then?' Ralph asked Maddy, putting his hands deep into his pockets.

'Oh, that there's a right time for everything.'

Ralph halted, looked at Maddy and laughed. Then together they walked over to where Ralph's mother was standing, waiting with the taxi that would take them home.

Also from Lion Publishing

MIDNIGHT BLUE

Pauline Fisk

Bonnie saw ropes hanging loose, poles falling away,
tree-tops sinking beneath her. As they rose, the sun rose
with them. Its warmth turned the dark skin of the fiery
balloon midnight blue. They flew straight up. Above
them, the sweet, clear music of the lonely pipe called to
them. Then the smooth sky puckered into cloth-of-blue
and drew aside. They passed straight through...

Winner of the Smarties Book Prize 1990

ISBN 0 7459 1925 1

THE 'PANGUR BÁN' SERIES

Fay Sampson

Six beautiful, exciting adventures set in the dramatic era of Celtic Britain.

SHAPE-SHIFTER: THE NAMING OF PANGUR BÁN
ISBN 0 7459 1347 4

PANGUR BÁN, THE WHITE CAT
ISBN 0 85648 580 2

FINNGLAS OF THE HORSES
ISBN 0 85648 899 2

FINNGLAS AND THE STONES OF CHOOSING
ISBN 0 7459 1124 2

THE SERPENT OF SENARGAD
ISBN 0 7459 1520 5

THE WHITE HORSE IS RUNNING
ISBN 0 7459 1915 4

THE LITTLE WHITE HORSE

Elizabeth Goudge

'For a fleeting instant Maria thought she saw a little white horse with a flowing mane and tail, head raised, poised, halted in mid-flight, as though it had seen her and was glad.'

The beautiful valley of Moonacre is shadowed by the memory of the Moon Princess and the mysterious little white horse. To her surprise Maria Merryweather, a stranger to Moonacre Manor, finds herself involved with what happened to the Moon Princess so many years before. She is determined to restore peace and happiness to the whole of Moonacre Valley. And Maria usually gets her way . . .

Elizabeth Goudge's many novels have achieved great popularity with readers of all ages. Judged to be an outstanding book for children, *The Little White Horse* was awarded the Carnegie Medal in 1946.

ISBN 0 7459 1458 6

More stories from LION PUBLISHING for you to enjoy:

MIDNIGHT BLUE Pauline Fisk	£2.99☐
LITTLE WHITE HORSE Elizabeth Goudge	£2.25☐
QUEST Dorothy Oxley	£2.25☐
SHAPE-SHIFTER Fay Sampson	£2.50☐
PANGUR BÁN Fay Sampson	£1.99☐
FINNGLAS OF THE HORSES Fay Sampson	£2.50☐
FINNGLAS AND THE STONES OF CHOOSING Fay Sampson	£2.25☐
SERPENT OF SENARGAD Fay Sampson	£2.25☐
THE WHITE HORSE IS RUNNING Fay Sampson	£2.50☐
OPERATION TITAN Dilwyn Horvat	£2.50☐
ASSAULT ON OMEGA FOUR Dilwyn Horvat	£2.50☐
STARFORCE RED ALERT Chris Spencer	£2.50☐

All Lion paperbacks are available from your local bookshop or newsagent, or can be ordered direct from the address below. Just tick the titles you want and fill in the form.

Name (Block letters) _____

Address_____

_____

Write to Lion Publishing, Cash Sales Department, PO Box 11, Falmouth, Cornwall TR10 9EN, England.

Please enclose a cheque or postal order to the value of the cover price plus:

UK: 80p for the first book, 20p for each additional book ordered to a maximum charge of £2.00.

OVERSEAS INCLUDING EIRE: £1.50 for the first book, £1.00 for the second book and 30p for each additional book.

BFPO: 80p for the first book, 20p for each additional book.

Lion Publishing reserves the right to show on covers and charge new retail prices which may differ from those previously advertised in the text or elsewhere, and to increase postal rates in accordance with the Post Office.